Shifter 5: Cole's Awakening

By
Jaden Sinclair

Shifters 5: Cole's Awakening

Published by
Melange Books, LLC
White Bear Lake, MN 55110
www.melange-books.com

Shifter 5, Cole's Awakening, Jaden Sinclair Copyright © 2009, 2011
ISBN 978-1-61235-031-8

Names, characters, and incidents depicted in this book are products of the author's imagination or are used fictitiously. Any resemblance to actual events, locales, organizations, or persons, living or dead, is entirely coincidental and beyond the intent of the author or the publisher. No part of this book may be reproduced or transmitted in any form or by any means, electronic or mechanical, including photocopying, recording, or by any information storage and retrieval system, without permission in writing from the publisher.

Credits:

Editor: Nancy Schumacher
Copy Editor: Taylor Evans
Format Editor: Mae Powers
Cover Artist: Caroline Andrus

Picture of male image used with permission from Marc Patton, model.

Shifter 5: Cole's Awakening
By
Jaden Sinclair

Celine Draeger has always wanted Cole Sexton, and knew he was her mate—she just didn't know how she would make him hers. His code of honor towards the family prevents him from staking a claim, so she decided to do one herself.

Cole fights within himself for the one he wants the most. No other will do for him but Celine. Only he can barely take care of himself, so how is he going to care for a mate? That is the question which prevents him from placing a claim on her. But when Celine takes matters into her own hands, Cole finds he can't refuse her anything.

The heat of the full moon has come, so hot it is guaranteed to ignite a fire to burn the soul. An awakening has begun. But who will be consumed by it?

* * * *

To Marc Patton: You made Cole come to life and there isn't anyone else that could have done it like you. Thank you so much for being on the cover, Jaden.

* * * *

www.jadensinclair.com

Shifter 5: Cole's Awakening
By
Jaden Sinclair

Prologue

Cole Sexton paced the upstairs hall of the Draeger home, his hands in his pockets worried about what was going to happen to him and his brother. He was only seventeen. He didn't know how the hell he was going to take care of his brother or himself, and he didn't like the idea of these people taking over either.

They were alone, true, but he didn't like the idea of taking a hand out. Even now he had to fight not to grab his brother and walk right out the front door.

His father had always told him to stand on his own two feet, to never take a hand out. He was a shifter. Be proud of that and if anything ever was to happen to him or his mother then he would be the one to look after Chase. Plain and simple.

And yet it wasn't that plain or simple. He couldn't take care of his brother, any more than he could take care of himself.

"Cole." He jumped, turning to frown when he heard Natasha Draeger. She stood at the foot of the stairs, a kind smile on her face. "Come in the dining room please."

She turned away. He swallowed hard, then he walked down the stairs slowly. They were all in there. He felt each one of their eyes on him. With their stares came a feeling, as though he was a small boy about to get into major trouble. The Draegers were a powerful family. One you wanted on your side.

"We can't let you and your brother leave unprotected," Dedrick Draeger said. He was a large man with dark hair and even darker eyes. He was the head of their family. "Stan knows your brother is alive and that has put a mark on his head."

"And before you say it," Drake butted in, putting his hand up so Cole wouldn't say anything, "You can't protect him like you think you can. *We* can."

"Then what do you want me to do?" Cole asked through clenched teeth. He tried to control his anger, but it must have shown.

Natasha came over to him, wrapping her arm around his shoulders. "I want you and your brother to come live with me."

Cole was speechless.

"It's the best thing," Dedrick went on. "You both can finish school and my mother will keep you safe."

"I can't do that," Cole whispered.

"Sure you can," Natasha said with a smile, rubbing his back. "Besides, I really don't want to be alone, and I can't stay here any longer. The girls need to run the house on their own, not with an old woman in the way."

"They never thought that." Stefan said.

She brushed them aside with a wave of her hand, "Needless to say, I want you boys to come with me."

"In other words, she wants someone to mother since we're all too old." Brock snickered.

Stefan slapped Brock on the back of the head. Natasha shook her head and slightly pushed Cole to a seat.

"The house is pretty large. Not as big as this one, but still too much for one person." She took his hand as he faced her. "I'm asking you Cole, not ordering. Please come and keep one old woman company for the rest of her years."

He looked around the room. Saw the concern in everyone's eyes, and knew when he met Natasha's eyes there was no way he could tell her no. This family had done so much for him. They had saved his brother's life. How could he refuse to give them the one thing they had asked in return?

"Okay," he sighed, nodding. "We'll move in."

Natasha smiled and kissed him on the cheek before hugging him tight.

Two Weeks Later

"So what do you think about all of this?" Cole asked his brother, Chase, who was resting back on one of the lounge chairs next to the pool.

He'd waited a week before telling Chase that they would be moving with Natasha. Cole was a bit surprised that his brother didn't get upset over it. Instead, Chase welcomed it with open arms, admitting that they needed the help, which Cole couldn't deny. As much as Cole hated to admit it, he knew that he couldn't protect Chase from the son-of-a-bitch who'd taken him.

Shifters 5: Cole's Awakening

"It's a new beginning, Cole," Chase answered, his eyes hidden behind dark sunglasses. "We need a fresh start."

Behind his own sunglasses, Cole glanced around the pool, at the family. Everyone was there, including Adrian, Skyler and their five kids, Alex, Ash, Fox, Darian, and Lyssa, making it one large ass barbecue. His eyes landed on someone he knew for a fact he shouldn't be staring at. He was damn glad he had his dark glasses on. Staring at her could get him killed in more ways than one.

Celine Draeger.

Now there was a girl who was going to be a knock out when she finished growing up and filling out. Cole pitied the poor bastard who ever thought about staking a claim on her. Dedrick would kill him. Plain and simple. Hell, he even felt sorry for the guy who would eventually try and date her. He couldn't see Dedrick letting his baby girl out of his sight or letting her go very easily.

"You know, I think you stare at her as much as she does you," Chase said.

Cole tore his eyes from her, sitting down in a lounge chair next to him. "I'm not staring, just thinking. Feel sorry for the guy who wants her." He stretched out, crossing his legs at the ankles. "Do you know what Dedrick will do to the poor bastard?" he chuckled. "Hate to be him, whoever he is."

"Why do you care?"

Cole frowned, linking his hands together, placing them over his head. "I don't," he sighed. "Just making conversation with you."

"Don't what?" Celine had walked up to them so quietly that he jumped when she spoke.

His eyes slowly went from her feet up her legs, waist—he had to close his eyes to stop there and open them back up on her face. She was only twelve, he reminded himself. Too young to be thinking about anything that didn't have to deal with friendship. *Just keep telling yourself that you like your nuts right where they are, then everything will be fine. Dedrick won't kill you if you don't mess with his daughter or think about her as a mate.*

"Nothing." He moved his legs fast when she sat down on the foot of the chair and handed Chase a glass of lemonade.

"Grandma is really happy that you two are going with her. I think she was worried about being lonely or something," she said.

"What about her family?" Chase inquired.

"Well you know," she took a drink of her own lemonade, "She isn't used to being in a house alone."

Her damn bikini isn't helping things or that long silky black hair he was dying to fist his hands into. She's twelve damn it! Cole felt like he was having an argument in his head, and strangely he was. He had his reasons, but something else was happening to him; something that bothered him. He hadn't experienced these thoughts the first time he saw her, so why now?

"So when is Natasha going to want to leave?" Cole asked, clearing his throat.

"I think this weekend," she answered. Then she smiled at him and it felt like a punch in his gut. "Why? Are you getting tired of me?"

He couldn't sit here. He had to get away from her. Cole didn't answer her, only stood up and walked away. When he glanced back at them, he saw her teasing Chase. It bothered him, and Cole knew it shouldn't. He was seventeen, she was only twelve. Celine was still a damn kid. One he had no business looking at or even thinking about.

When she pushed at Chase, playing around with him, Cole watched the two of them with envy. Chase was more her age. It should be him thinking about Celine, wondering what was going on and why he had so much interest. But it wasn't Chase, it was Cole standing in the open watching his brother tease the girl whom Cole had to keep at a distance. Too young and a father who would kill. He needed no more reminders.

He jumped when Dedrick and Drake splashed into the pool. Cole got tense all over and was unable to shake it off. He watched the playfulness between Dedrick and Drake. Saw the teasing and joking of Chase with Celine, the loving way that Brock treated Heather and even how Adrian, and Stefan, teased each other in front of their mates. A real family, this was what was going on all around him. He missed being part of a family, and yet he felt like a stranger standing on the outside looking in. His feelings were so confused. Everyone around him had something that he didn't. Everyone was at ease, and he was tense, feeling out of place. Chase was at home here, but Cole didn't feel it. Something was missing and he either couldn't see it or was fighting what was right in front of him.

"You okay?" Natasha asked, touching his arm, startling him.

Cole put on what he hoped was a convincing smile and nodded. He glanced over his shoulder, biting the inside of his mouth to stop the growl, which was forming from slipping past his lips. Chase was standing, backing Celine up. She had her hands up to ward him off, laughing. The way they were standing had the hairs on the back of his neck standing, the instinct to charge over there was unbelievably strong.

He didn't answer Natasha. He just turned away from her and started walking, then he moved into the house at a jog, and up the steps to his bedroom. Once the door was closed, he groaned and rubbed his face, breathing fast and hard. He was so tense he couldn't think straight. Didn't even notice he was moving until he was standing next to the window watching the family—watching his brother and Celine. *Twelve dammit!*

"Cole?" Natasha's cool voice seemed to calm his nerves that were quickly rising and threatening to burn him. He didn't understand where these feelings were coming from or why his eyes were following a girl he had no business watching. "Want to talk about it?"

He shook his head, "Not really."

"Does this have to do with you moving?"

He rubbed his eyes and forced himself to turn and face her. "No. I'm just tired, that's all."

The tenderness in her face was enough to make him feel as if he should be wallowing in guilt. He'd just lied to her because he couldn't tell her what was wrong. Hell, *he* didn't even know what was wrong with him.

"Okay. But if you need to talk, I'm here." He nodded at her and grinned in acknowledgement. "I might surprise you with what I know."

She had him speechless when she left him alone. He was worried, with one question that came to mind, did she know? Could she tell by his behavior that something wasn't right and that it might have to do with Celine? God, he hoped not. That was all he'd need—for Dedrick to come after his ass for no reason but looking at his daughter.

"Why do I have this feeling that I am so damn fucked?" he groaned before dropping face down on the bed where he could yell his frustrations into the bedding and not have to worry about anyone overhearing him.

* * * *

Four years later

Sixteen. She was sixteen now and a knock out. There was no way in *hell* she was going to stay without a mate for much longer. Cole joined the family for a surprise sweet sixteen birthday celebration for Celine and when she came in with her parents Cole thought his mouth was going to drop open. He sure as hell felt embarrassment because of the way his body came to life just looking at her. *Still too young, you asshole!*

Natasha forced him to come along, tossing the family thing in his face. It was her favorite line when she wanted him to do something family orientated. He tried to get out of it, telling her that it was his last year in college and he really needed to study for finals, but she wouldn't give in to his excuses. And the way she would smile at him made him think that she knew something he didn't. Was there another reason why he was being dragged to the family get-togethers and not Chase? Lucky Chase was doing finals.

But for this occasion, this birthday, he had tried even harder to get out of it. He didn't want to have to go through what he went through four years ago, and that was just what he was doing now, only this time it was even worse. The second he saw her, his gut twisted and he got that strange possessive feeling again.

Cole knew that he shouldn't have this feeling. He was twenty-one to her sweet sixteen. Kid. Adult. Could it get any clearer?

After he said his hellos, answered the how are you doing questions, he made an excuse and left to get some air. Cole couldn't watch her smile and laugh and act like nothing was bothering him. He couldn't be close with the temptation of touching forbidden fruit.

"You're fighting it." He turned his head and there stood Stefan. "I see it in your eyes. In the way you walk and tense up."

"Excuse me?"

Stefan walked up to him handed him a beer and motioned with his head to follow him to the patio, to a table and chairs. He sat down and Cole followed suit.

"I've been there," Stefan went on. "Felt it and had to wait before I was able to do a damn thing about it. Sidney was too young to claim." He took a drink. "Man those years were a bitch."

"What makes you think that's my problem?" He also took a drink, kept his eyes on Stefan and tried like hell to act like nothing was wrong. He must have failed because Stefan gave him a big smile.

"Well either you are trying to fight it, or you don't want the girl." Stefan sat back and put his feet on the table, crossing his ankles. "Which is it?"

Cole took a long draw from his beer, enjoying the slight burn that went down his throat. "Neither." He sounded strained when he spoke and when one eyebrow went up on Stefan's face he knew that the man wasn't buying it.

"How young is she?"

Cole put his beer on the table slowly and lowered his eyes. "What makes you think it's a girl?"

"Well, Ma told me—"

"Natasha's telling you things about me now." He couldn't keep the accusation from his voice. "I don't believe this!"

"Now don't get your ass all up in a bind. She only told me that dating hasn't been your thing. She suspects that you have found your mate but are reluctant to make a move on her." He cocked his head to the side, staring at Cole. "And the way you're acting right now, I'm going to have to agree with her."

"Is that so?"

"And she thinks it's someone in the family," Stefan added.

"Fuck," Cole groaned and pushed away from the table. He stood up and walked away. Surprisingly, Stefan didn't follow him but stayed at the table drinking his beer.

"Would you tell me if it was?" Stefan asked, stopping Cole from going back into the house.

Cole turned around; his brows pulled together, eyes narrowed. "Stefan, there isn't anything to tell. I don't have a mate; don't know who she is, and no, if I did, I probably wouldn't say anything to you guys but I'd ship my ass off and get the hell away from here. I wouldn't disrespect you all by doing something like that."

Stefan stood up, beer in hand. He walked up to Cole, standing face to face. "I'm only going to say this once. You could never disrespect us by claiming one of our own as your mate. You don't owe us anything Cole. So stop thinking that you do." He took a deep breath, letting it out slowly. "To disrespect us, is to deny a gift that is standing right in front of you. If by chance one of our girls is your mate, don't fuck it up. That," he pointed his finger at him, "Would get your ass kicked." He smiled, slapping Cole on the shoulder. "Now let's get some cake before Drake eats half of it."

Stefan left and Cole sighed. Stefan did have a point. He'd known the family long enough to know that if he didn't take action and messed it up, they would kick his ass. And that was a lot of Draegers to go through.

His peace came to an end, his body tensed and a faint sweet scent came with the wind, slapping him gently in the face. He closed his eyes, taking as much of it into his lungs, holding it there. It gave him a sense of calm just like it brought forth a hunger inside him that he knew was going to get him into a whole hell of a lot of trouble.

"There you are!" Celine's voice—and boy did it do things to him that it had no business doing to him. He turned on the heels of his feet and tried to smile, but failed.

Celine was dressed in a yellow thin-strapped dress that hugged each and every one of her curves. Her coal black hair was loose, hanging to the middle of her back and when the wind blew softly her hair brushed over her young chest and the skirt hugged her legs. She looked so much like Jaclyn with the long hair and slim figure, but her features had the darkness of the shifter side and of Dedrick. Thinking about Dedrick helped to remind him of her age and to keep his eyes on her face. She had her mother's eyes. They were so blue that he found himself wanting to get lost in them. Hell, he knew for a fact he could stare at her all night long and never get tired of it.

"They're about to bring out the cake." She smiled and his heart pounded in his chest. "If you want some before Drake, you better get in there."

He tried to smile, but failed. Cole couldn't seem to act normal with her, could only stare. Without thinking, he reached down and touched her cheek, moving back to put a lock of hair behind her ear. "You've grown up." He dropped his hand before he was tempted to touch more, cleared his throat, and reached inside his jacket pocket for the small box—her present. "Here," he handed it to her. "Happy birthday."

She smiled big right before she ripped the paper and opened the box. Inside was a heart necklace with a small heart shaped diamond in the middle. He had it especially made for her, even though she never took off the locket that Drake had given her years ago.

Her face lit up and the smile she gave him stole his breath away. "I love it," she breathed out.

She handed it to him and turned her back towards him, picking up her thick hair and moving it over her shoulders. Cole's mouth went dry looking down at her skin. Her skin was so creamy, so soft looking it had his hands shaking while he clasped the necklace around her neck, over the locket.

Celine took one step away, head down and turned back around to face him. She was looking at the heart. "You know for the past few years I had hoped you would come for one of my birthdays, but grandma always said you were too busy with school."

"Yeah, um," he cleared his throat, feeling very uncomfortable. "I have finals I need to study for, but Natasha dragged me here. Um, we should go inside. You did say that—"

Celine took two steps closer, grabbed the front of his shirt, pulled him down to her level and kissed him. Cole's first reaction was to let go and give into the kiss, and he was about to do just that. Had his arms starting to go around her to hold her closer, when that inner voice of his yelled again. *Sixteen you dumb ass!*

The kiss ended and Cole stood there, stunned, not sure what to do or say. Of all the things he might have expected her to do, that was definitely not one of them.

"Thank you," she whispered, her lips so close he could nip on them. "I love the necklace.

He watched her leave, forced himself to stay there and let her go. Still too young, but very dangerous. That was what Celine Draeger had become. She was Jaclyn all over, and if what he had heard about how Dedrick and Jaclyn got together was true, then Cole was in major trouble. He sensed that she was too much like her mother, and if that was true then who ever Celine set her sights on—well there was going to be one hell of a dilemma in the Draeger household he had a feeling. His gut of his was screaming that he was going to be right dab in the middle of it.

"Why is this happening to me?" he groaned, running a hand into his hair. He took several deep breaths, but it didn't work. "I'm fucked. I'm definitely fucked here and there isn't going to be a damn thing anyone can do," he blew loudly. "Yep. I'm a dead man."

Five years later

"Mr. Sexton?"

Cole was sitting out in the waiting room of the hospital. Natasha had collapsed again and this time she didn't get up. In fact, she'd passed out in the kitchen when he found her, scaring the shit out of him.

For months, she had been sick, but trying to hide it. Cole knew, and when she figured out he knew she conned him into *not* saying anything to the family. She didn't want them all to head here taking over.

He jumped up when the doctor approached him and shook hands. "How is she?"

A grim expression on the man's face said it all. "She's suffered a stroke and a heart attack. It doesn't look good." Cole thought he was going to be sick. "She's asking for you and I think it would be best if you call her family. This stroke with the heart attack has done a number on her. She only has thirty percent of her heart functioning and her organs are shutting down."

Cole nodded and followed the doctor into her room. Natasha was sleeping in the bed, oxygen over her mouth and IVS and heart monitors were hooked up to her body. The sight was unnerving. She looked older and weaker, not the strong woman that he had spent so many years living with.

She knew he was in the room. Her smile told him that. Natasha opened her eyes and motioned to him with her hand to come over. He did, taking her hand and sitting down on the side of the bed.

Cole couldn't help himself and leaned over, resting his face on her chest, hugging her. He closed his eyes when she also moved her arm, to hold him weakly.

"I'm not ready to let you go," he whispered. "I'm not ready to be alone."

"Not…alone."

He raised his head, tears falling from his eyes. "I know I have Chase, but you—"

She moved her hand and touched his cheek, silencing him. "Don't…fight…it." She took a deep breath. "You'll…lose…" she sighed, hand dropping and eyes closing.

The heart monitor went off and all Cole could do was lower his face back to her chest and cry softly. Natasha Draeger was gone.

Chapter One

Cole stood out in the freezing rain one week later, with the Draeger family saying his last good-byes to Natasha Draeger. It took a whole week for the family to come together and, in that time, Cole thought about the last words she gave him. *Don't fight it.* He didn't understand what she was talking about. Don't fight what? He somewhat had an idea of what she might be talking about but shook it off. No one knew, he'd made extra sure of it. Dressed in his best, head bowed, he thought about it while the priest spoke the final words as her coffin was lowered into the ground next to her husband.

For ten years, one girl he had no business thinking about was always on his mind. Cole refused to think of her as his. She was out of his reach, and he was going to keep it that way. So even if Natasha's words were meant to encourage him not to fight the desire that was ever present when Celine was around, Cole wasn't going to listen. He wasn't going to do the family that way. Never!

Natasha wasn't his and Chase's mother but they both loved her as if she were. And to stand here saying his silent good-bye was so very painful, just like watching her body being lowered into the grave. It felt like he was burying his own parents all over again, and that damn feeling of being alone was present once more.

Each of the Draegers stepped forward one by one to toss a handful of dirt on top of her casket. In his hand, he held a single red rose. A tear slipped from his eye when he let it go to land on the dirt. His eyes locked on where it landed. What was he going to do now?

"Man, thou art dust and to dust thou shall return." The priest recited as he continued the service. He made the sign of the cross over the casket, and then he blessed all of the family. "May she rest in peace."

He looked up to the family, but his eyes landed on Celine Draeger. She was all grown up now at twenty-one, knocking what little breath he had right out of his chest. Like everyone else around the gravesite, she was dressed in black with a coat on and an umbrella over her head to protect her from the cold rain. Her long, waist length black hair hung loose with some of the strands blowing across her face with the wind. She definitely was Jaclyn Draeger's daughter.

Cole looked away before their eyes could meet. He'd never forgotten the kiss she gave him, or how it made him feel. And with those feelings and the urges and desires constantly hitting him, Cole made the decision, again, to stay away from her. It was the only respectable thing to do. All of this because of the one little kiss which started something that still affected him.

Because of that damn kiss, he couldn't date like he needed to. Couldn't get serious with any girl, because he would compare them to her, and for the past five years he sure as hell couldn't get laid. That meant he was a walking hard-on most of the time. *Don't fight it.*

"Hey, how you doing?" Drake came up to him and he jumped, snapping out of his thoughts to shake the hand that he'd held out in front of him. The group was breaking away and the Draeger family was coming up to him and Chase.

"I'm okay." Cole took a deep breath and cleared his throat. Now was not the time to be thinking about Natasha's last words to him or the best kiss of his life. "Guess I never thought Natasha would die, you know? And it happened so fast."

Drake pulled Cole into his arms and hugged him. Cole closed his eyes and welcomed the embrace. "Remember you're not alone. Okay?"

Cole nodded and stepped out of his arms, sniffing back the tears. Drake hugged Chase, while Cole steeled himself for the rest of the family.

Shifters 5: Cole's Awakening

"How you doing, kid?" Stefan asked with his usual smile in place.

"Hanging in there." Cole shook Stefan's hand, then turned his attention to Dedrick. Just the sight of the big man had his mouth drying up. If he knew that all Cole could think about the past few months was his daughter he knew his nuts would be ripped out. "The lawyer wants to see you today."

"Shit," Dedrick sighed. "Bastard can't even wait a day. We just buried our mother for Christ's sake."

"He told me that Natasha wanted the will read right after she was buried." Cole shrugged. "I'm just passing the information along."

Dedrick growled then headed for the limo. Cole and the rest of the family followed. They all got into the long limo and he cast a quick glance at Celine. *Get a grip on yourself,* he thought. *She just lost her grandmother, you dick, and doesn't need you to be thinking about touching her legs or kissing her.*

The limo driver drove them to Natasha's house on Cape Cod where not only friends but distant family members were waiting with food. The lawyer as well.mCole and Chase took everyone's coat and told them where they were to meet the lawyer. They were heading for a guest room where all the coats were when Jaclyn found them.

"The lawyer says you two are to come also," she told them.

Chase frowned at Cole before turning to her, "Why?"

"No idea." She shrugged.

They followed her out of the guest room and into the library. Dedrick, Stefan, Adrian, Sidney, Jaclyn and Skyler were seated in the available chairs, so they went over to the back corner to stand.

The lawyer looked around the room before clearing his throat and taking a seat. "Good, everyone's here. Now we can begin." He cleared his throat again before bringing out the will. "My dear family, I know this has come as a shock. I didn't want to tell any of you that I was sick. Knowing that my time could be up any moment I went and purchased a large amount of property in the Denver Mountains. Over three hundred acres and I had a home built there. The home is for Drake and his family, since Brock is busy with Heather and the company. Twenty acres of this land is to go to Cole and another twenty to Chase for homes of their own."

Cole's mouth dropped open.

"I have started college funds for each of my grandchildren. The home that you are standing in now, I give to my daughter and her family. The house that Stefan and Dedrick are in is now theirs as well." The lawyer put the paper down and looked up at them. "Your mother wanted me to read

Shifters 5: Cole's Awakening

this as soon as the funeral was over. She had everything signed over and finalized."

"No," Cole snapped, getting the attention of everyone in the room. "She can't do that!" He pushed off the wall and left the room before anyone could say anything.

"Cole, wait up!" Adrian was the one to follow him and Cole didn't know if that was good or bad. Adrian grabbed hold of his arm stopped and pulled him out to the porch.

"She promised me that she was never going to do anything like that," Cole said before anything else could be said. "Everything she had was to go to her family, not us!"

Adrian cocked his head to the side and stared at him. "Natasha looked on you two as family." He sniffed at Cole, which made him very uncomfortable. "How long has it been?"

"What?" Cole frowned.

"How long has it been since you've been with a woman?" He leaned in and sniffed closer. "The full moon was a week ago, but you still have it lingering. That only means one thing."

Cole backed away from him and moved to the other side of the porch. "I don't know what you're talking about, man."

Adrian put his hands in his pockets and swung around on the balls of his feet. "Been there, done that, remember? I had to wait six months before I could finish my claim. Does she know yet?"

Cole hung his head. He was about to deny it. Adrian was giving him a look that said no one with an ounce of sense should try to bullshit with a bullshitter, and Adrian was definitely a bullshitter. "No one knows, okay." He quickly looked him straight in the eye. "And I want to keep it that way."

Adrian's eyes narrowed and Cole held his breath. "Son-of-a-bitch," he whispered. "Don't tell me it's one of my girls."

Cole shook his head no and turned his back on Adrian.

"Cole?"

"Adrian please, I don't want—" Adrian grabbed his arm and forced him back to face him.

"If your mate is who I think she is then you do the right thing and don't fuck this up. You go talk to him about a claim!" Adrian spoke softly, but the seriousness of what he was saying was in his voice. "This is serious, man!"

Cole said nothing.

"Damn it, Cole," Adrian growled, let go of his arm and rubbed his face.

"Look, just keep your mouth shut." He ran a hand into his hair, looking around to make sure the rest of the family wasn't about to come out and overhear what they were talking about. "I'm not going to make a claim. I'm going to stay away and it will just go away."

"*This* doesn't go away," Adrian growled low. "It only gets worse, and if you don't believe me then ask Dedrick." Cole made the mistake of glancing at Adrian before looking away at the dark sky. "No way!"

"Adrian, don't."

"Are you shitting me?! Celine?" he pointed behind him.

Cole rubbed his face with both hands and groaned loudly. "Can you please say it a bit louder? I'm not sure if they all heard you!" He put one hand on his hip and paced the porch a couple of times, rubbing the back of his neck before stopping in front of Adrian. "I need you to keep this quiet."

Adrian chuckled, "You've got to be kidding me."

"No, I'm not." Cole grabbed at his tie, pulling it down. "I'd like to keep my nuts right where they are, thank you very fucking much."

"Shit," Adrian snickered. "You're really scared of him."

"Wouldn't you be if you were in my shoes?" he tossed back. He started pacing again, trying to figure out a way out of this mess. "Adrian, what the hell am I going to do?"

"Talk to Dedrick," Adrian answered, crossing his arms over his chest. Cole stopped to stare at Adrian who only shrugged his shoulders. "Only thing you can do."

Cole shook his head, "I need to think." He walked away from Adrian, back into the house and up the stairs, two at a time. By the time he reached his bedroom door he had the top four buttons of his shirt undone. He went right over to his bed and lay down, putting his hands up to cover his face.

"I'm sure there is a very good reason why you have been avoiding me." He sat up quickly when he heard her voice and tried like hell to act normal. But it was hard when he looked over at the door and it was still closed. That meant she was waiting in his room for him. Not good.

She pushed off the wall, her arms crossed over her chest. He swallowed hard and sat up slowly. "What are you doing in here?" Boy, talking was a bitch at the moment.

Remember, asshole, you like the nuts between your legs, not shoved down your throat! That damn black dress of hers barely touched her knees and was sinfully snug. It was plain and simple with long sleeves, but on her, it looked like something that should be banned. Her black heels drew all his attention to her enticing legs, giving him a mental picture of them wrapped around his hips. *Get a damn grip, or get laid!* It had been five years since he'd last seen her, and in that time she had turned out to be something exquisite. Damn if he wasn't in some serious trouble here.

"Waiting for you," She sighed, walking around his room, looking at things and touching some of his stuff. She picked up a photo on his dresser and cocked her head as she stared at it. "Is this your girlfriend?"

He moved from the bed towards her and snatched the photo from her hand, "Ex." He put it in a drawer and turned around to say something but stopped short. Words seemed to slip from his mind and all he could do was stand there. Celine was so close he could smell her scent and feel her body heat.

"Most guys toss the pictures of their ex," Her blue eyes captivated him and he had to shake it off. "She must have been special."

He cleared his throat and moved around her, only because he knew that if he stood there facing her he would do something stupid, like kiss her. "No, she wasn't. So why are you here?" he asked again, only because he didn't want her to see what she was doing to him. The control he had was slipping and he couldn't get it back. He went back over to the bed, sitting down. It was the only thing he could think to do. When he glanced back at her, a knot formed in the back of his throat. Celine was gorgeous. How the hell was he going to keep the proper distance? How the fuck was he going to stay away when all he wanted to do was claim her right this minute?

"Daddy said you left right after the will was read and you seemed upset." She went to the window and his eyes followed, roaming over her backside. When his eyes landed on her ass, his cock began to rise. He groaned and tried to hide it when she turned around. "I wanted to make sure you were all right."

He closed his eyes and tried to force it down, but couldn't. Five years of no sex was finally coming back to bite him in the ass. "I'm fine." Nope, he didn't sound fine, he sounded uptight.

"You don't sound fine to me."

Cole closed his eyes and took several deep breaths. She was close—too close. In fact she sat down on the bed next to him. He could smell her and it was quickly driving him nuts. *Someone help me!*

"You sound like something is very wrong." She touched his hair and his damn cock began to throb painfully. *Motherfucker!*

He made the mistake of turning around. She was so close, her lips mere inches from his. One small move and he could be kissing her,

Shifters 5: Cole's Awakening

touching her, having her under him. God to feel her skin as he wanted. To taste her—oh shit he needed to get away from her and he needed to do it right now!

"You look like you want to kiss me." She inched closer, her voice a low whispered of softness that seemed to touch his skin. "Do you?"

God yes! "This isn't right." Before he could make a mistake, Cole stood up and as fast as he could to leave his room. Cole shook his head, just about jumped half of the stairs to get down them. He had to get away from her. If he didn't something bad was going to happen. Something that he wouldn't be able to fix or take back. Celine deserved to have the kind of guy who could give her the world. Cole didn't have that. He wasn't right for Celine. Hell he didn't know in what direction he was going. He also knew that her father wasn't going to give her up without a fight.

Dedrick and Jaclyn had waited so long to have a child. It took ten years after she had a miscarriage to get pregnant again. No one was ever good enough for Celine. Drake even told him that if the wrong guy came along he would help Dedrick show the bastard to the door. She was very tight with Brock and Drake. Between the three men, Celine was practically a nun when it came to dating. Between those three it was no wonder that she was still unclaimed and untouched.

He didn't say anything to Drake or Dedrick who were standing next to the door talking, and he should have. He should if for no other reason than to keep the front going that nothing was wrong. They stopped talking and stared at him. Cole lowered his eyes as he yanked the front door open. He welcomed the cold rain with a sigh and closed his eyes. He was on fire and couldn't seem to get the burn to cool.

Cole walked around to the back of the house. He headed right for the spot he had set up for his workouts. A homemade bar was screwed between two trees so he and Chase could do chin-ups. It helped him to work out, during his heat it curbed his sexual needs, which he appeared to be suffering from right now thanks to Celine's little visit to his room. Thinking about who would be the first one to beat the holy hell out of him once his lust for Celine was discovered, helped get his erection to start going down. The chin ups and the cold rain took care of the rest.

He gripped the wet, slippery bar and started to work out. He lost count and track of time, just like he always did when he was working off the burn. His only focus was to get the thoughts of Celine to go away, no matter how much pain he went through. He had to get a grip, had to get through this until she left to go back home.

"One twenty and counting," Drake remarked, strolling out in the open for Cole to see. "Impressive."

Cole stopped midway up and glanced at Drake, "What's wrong?"

"I think I should be asking you that question." Drake crossed his arms over his chest and leaned back against the house. "Uncle Adrian hinted that something was wrong and that I should come out here and talk to you."

Cole dropped to the ground. He was a bit labored in his breathing. Even though it was only drizzling, he looked like a drowned rat because his chest was covered in sweat. "Adrian's wrong. I'm fine."

"Un-huh," Drake nodded. "Bullshit someone else please. What's wrong?"

Cole shook his head, wiping his arm over his wet face. "Nothing."

"Then why the hell are you out here doing chin ups in the damn rain? We only do stupid shit like that when we are either in heat or…"

Cole's mouth went dry and a chill raced down his spine. "It's nothing. I'm fine." He quickly interrupted.

Drake raised his head, but lowered his eyes on Cole. "Adrian doesn't butt in to shit unless something's up. What's going on, Cole?"

"It's just been a very stressful day."

Drake took a deep breath and let it out slowly. "Bullshit."

Cole groaned and rubbed his face, and raked his fingers into his long wet hair. "Drake, I don't want to have this out with you right now. I just want to be left alone."

"Have what out with me? What the hell is that supposed to mean?"

"Drake…"

Drake held up his hand, silencing him, "It isn't me you need to worry about, it's Dedrick. *I'm* not the one going to rip your nuts off and feed them to you."

Cole's mouth dropped open. He was shocked. Not just by what Drake said but with the cautious manner in which he said it. "How…how…"

"Dad figured it out years ago and told me then. Thought I might want to choke you or something." He shrugged like this all didn't bother him or matter that much. "But we didn't tell Uncle Dedrick because he's different than me when it comes to her. He *would* have choked you back then."

"Does everyone know?" Cole asked through his teeth.

"Not everyone." He scratched the side of face and wore a confused expression. "But I must say I'm a little surprised. Didn't see this one coming and I normally always do." He slid his hands into his pockets and cocked his head to one side. "When are you going to tell him and make your claim?"

"I'm not."

Now it was Drake's turn for the mouth to drop. "Are you out of your mind?"

"I think I am for having this conversation with *you*!"

"You don't tell Dedrick and this blows out of your control…he might kill you then."

"You are just full of great advice." Cole couldn't keep the bitterness from his voice. "And for your information I've done great for ten damn years."

"Ten!" Drake gasped. "You've known this shit for ten years? That would've made her—"

"Twelve." Cole remarked dryly when Drake started to count.

Drake whispered, "Damn. That's a long time to keep this a secret." He bit his lower lip, then nodded. "Okay. Let's go talk to him." Cole opened his mouth to argue that but didn't get a chance to speak.

"Who's that?" Drake asked.

Cole glanced around Drake to see a young woman who could give Celine a run for her money with the term gorgeous. Even in jeans and a baggy sweater one could make out a body any male of his race would hunger for. She had medium length brown hair, a short frame and if his memory served him right, green eyes that sparkled like emeralds. She was also a full blooded human, with a temper to match any shifter female. Cole tended to stay away from her whenever the spitfire came around. Because like him and Chase, she didn't have much family. She didn't like to talk about her family, and Chase didn't push to know.

"That would be Jada. Jada Leonard, she's Chase's friend," he said stunned, only because he didn't know why she would be here. "I'll be back." He met her halfway up the walk. "What's up, Jada?"

"I need to see Chase," she answered with her head to the side and tilted up at him.

She was definitely shorter than Celine, only coming up to the middle of his chest, but Cole knew for a fact Jada could handle herself. Somehow, his brother became friends with her and she learned their secret. It was a little detail he kept forgetting to find out from his brother. He didn't know Jada very well, and he wasn't sure yet if he could trust her or not.

"He's inside I think."

She nodded and licked her lips before digging into her pocket and handing him a roll of film, "Give him this."

Cole looked down and took it from her. "What is it?"

"Information," she answered. "It's on a need to know basis, and at the moment, that's all you need to know."

She turned to leave but Cole grabbed her arm, stopping her. "What's he got you doing this time?"

Jada jerked her arm free and glared up at him. "You ever stop and think I help Chase because I like him?" Her eyes went up and down his body. "Unlike you, he's nice."

Cole let her go but stood rooted to the spot until she was out of sight.

"And what was that all about?" Drake asked, coming up next to him.

"No idea." He tossed the film up in the air and Drake caught it. "But Chase should know."

* * * *

"You did what?" Cole couldn't stop yelling at his brother, as he wore a path pacing in the study. Drake dragged him in to talk to Dedrick, but he ended up yelling at his brother instead. Cole needed to know what Jada Leonard was giving Chase, *not* talk about a claiming that wasn't going to happen. What Chase told him had Cole seeing red. "How could you bring a human into this mess?"

"She's sneaky," Chase defended. "She can find information on just about anything."

Cole growled and fisted his hands in his hair.

"Calm down, Cole," Dedrick sighed. "So what has she found out?"

Chase sat forward in his seat and took a deep breath. At twenty-one, it was obvious Chase was going to be as big of a shifter male as any of them. He had the same hazel eyes as his brother, but his hair was lighter brown, almost a sandy brown at times.

"Their names," Chase answered. "And a few pictures."

"Whose names?" Dedrick asked.

Chase took a deep breath and Cole found he was holding his. "When I was in that cage I saw them both. And some guy who got off on torturing the boy. I don't know who they are or where they came from, but I made that boy a promise to get him out one day, if I didn't die first."

"You made a promise," Cole sighed.

"And I'm going to keep it," Chase stood up.

"How well can you trust this girl?" Drake asked.

"Jada and I have an understanding," Chase answered. "I trust her to keep what we are a secret as well as trust her to help get this information for us."

"I don't know about this, Stefan," Dedrick mumbled loud enough for them all to hear.

"So what do you two know then?" Stefan asked with his arms crossed over his chest. He leaned back against the counter in a lazy manner, listening quietly.

Chase glanced at Cole, then, even though Chase thought his gut was going to drop, he turned to face Stefan, "More than you guys know."

"Shit!" Cole hissed under his breath. "Why the hell have you kept this from us?"

"Because I knew you wouldn't let me help!" Chase charged back. "I was in that cage and *I* know what the hell has been going on better than any of you."

"Everyone calm down," Dedrick snapped. He turned to Cole. "Chase has a right to help." When Cole opened his mouth to rebut it, Dedrick went on and cut him off. "He has firsthand knowledge of this shit and apparently he's getting better information than any of us at the moment."

"I'm waiting to hear what you know." Drake was acting way too cool in the kitchen. It didn't set well with Cole at all, not when a few minutes ago he was teasing Cole about Celine.

"So far what we've discovered is the male is all shifter and the female is all human."

"A female?" Stefan butted in.

"They're twins, but born at different times. Five or six years apart, maybe more." Chase responded.

"Is that possible?" Cole frowned.

"It is if you freeze the egg after it splits," Drake grumbled.

Chase nodded. "Jada gave me photos of some medical reports she saw on them. She called me last week with names as well." He glanced around the room at everyone. "He has named himself Kane and he calls her Sasha."

"And he's shifter," Drake commented.

"And she's all human," Chase added, getting Drake's full attention. "They were also created, and born from a test tube somehow. She thinks that later on they were inserted into someone, but she hasn't found that information out yet."

"Any idea?" Stefan asked.

Chase shook his head. "No, and this Josh Stan keeps moving them around."

"Stan?" Stefan pushed off the wall he'd been leaning back against. "Josh Stan is in charge of this shit?"

Chase nodded. "And a Jason Spencer is like babysitting them."

"Fuck!" Dedrick groaned. He turned to Stefan. "I told you I should have ripped that bastard's throat out."

"Well it just keeps getting better and better," Drake sighed.

"So what now?" Cole asked, crossing his arms over his chest.

Dedrick opened his mouth, but Drake cut him off. "There is something else that needs to be discussed.

Cole shook his head 'no' quickly. "Shut up Drake." he said through this teeth.

"Like what?" Dedrick frowned, glancing quickly at Cole before fixing those dark eyes of his on Drake.

"Like—" Cole rushed up on Drake and covered his mouth with his hand, but Drake pulled him off. "Uncle Adrian, hold him."

Adrian grabbed Cole's arm and Stefan took hold of the other one, pulling him away from Drake.

"Damn it, Drake, shut the fuck up," Cole snapped.

"What the hell is going on?" Dedrick demanded, his hands on his hips. With his wide stance he appeared ready to pounce on someone, and Cole was thinking that someone was going to be him real soon if Drake didn't keep his mouth shut.

"It's Celine," Stefan sighed, struggling with Cole. "She has a mate and he's a bit hesitant about approaching you for the claim."

Dedrick's eyes narrowed on Cole and he knew he was seeing death in the big man's eyes.

"Now don't over react—" Drake started to say, but was too late.

Dedrick growled and lunged at Cole. Adrian and Stefan let him go and grabbed hold of Dedrick before he could get his hands on him.

"Now do you understand why I wanted you to keep your damn mouth shut!" Cole yelled at Drake. "Now do you get why I don't want to do this!"

"Dedrick, he's like family now. You can't kill him." Stefan said, grunting as he held onto Dedrick.

"Oh, I'm not going to kill him, just squeeze some of the life out of him."

"And here I thought he overreacted with me and Skyler," Adrian added.

"Not helping," Stefan groaned.

Dedrick broke free. His hands went around Cole's neck and he slammed him up against the wall. Cole didn't stop him or fight him, but met his stare, showing that he wasn't going to fight or back down.

"How long, Cole," Dedrick spoke low and deadly, putting enough pressure on his throat to cut some of his air off. "How long have you lusted after my daughter?"

"I've...I haven't lusted..." More pressure was placed on his throat making Cole think he was going to pass out. "Ten," he struggled to answer.

Dedrick stilled, his eyes widened and he let go of his throat. He took one step back, dropped his arms and Cole reached up to rub his throat. Without warning Dedrick sucker punched him in the jaw, knocking him to the ground.

"Then you should have fucking told me." Dedrick turned around. "I'll be in the kitchen."

"That went surprisingly well," Adrian snickered.

"Damn, he can hit hard." Cole moved so he was sitting on his ass on the floor and rubbed his jaw. He tasted blood and when he touched his lip, his fingers came away red.

Drake knelt down in front of him with a smile. "Now go have a beer with him and make nice." Cole took his hand to get back up. "The worst part is over."

"I don't think I want to go in the kitchen with him." Cole rubbed his jaw. "There're knives in there."

Drake turned him and gave him a push. "Tough."

Cole frowned and looked over his shoulder. "I really don't want—"

"Go!" Adrian, Stefan and Drake yelled together.

But he couldn't go. Instead, he shook his head. "I can't do this guys. I'm sorry."

* * * *

Celine watched Cole leave the house. She flinched when he slammed the front door. She'd heard what had happened and it almost made her want to cry over it. She knew Cole was her mate. Knew it, told Drake and Brock about it, even her mother. But her mother told her to not push it, that if she pushed too hard it would only backfire on her. What she needed to do was talk to her father. This was just what she was going to do.

She pushed away from the corner she was hiding in and went to the kitchen. Her father was sitting at the table, drinking a beer.

"You hit him." It was a statement, not a question, one which had Dedrick stop before taking a drink, the bottle close to his lips.

"Yeah I did."

He took his drink, and she moved to the table, sitting down across from him. "Why?"

"Why didn't you tell me?" he tossed back at her, slamming his beer on the table and sitting back. "You couldn't tell me this?"

"I didn't want you to over react."

"Damn it, Celine." Dedrick pushed away from the table, standing up. "Now you sound like your mother."

"Well, look what happened," she charged back, stopping him from walking out. "If I would have told you when I suspected, you would have told me it was nothing more than a childish crush. In fact, I tried to tell you then," she pointed her finger at him. "You blew me off."

"Do you realize what this all means?" he growled at her. "If he wanted to make a claim, he would be in here talking to me, not you."

"And if you weren't so much of a bear, scaring everyone off, he might just have done that!" her voice rose, but she quickly calmed down, and stood up. "Daddy, please." She went up to him, wrapping her arms around his waist, hugging him tight. Dedrick put his arms around her as well. "I've loved him since I was twelve."

"What do you want me to do?" he sighed, sounding defeated.

She took a deep breath before stepping out of his arms to look up at him. "I want to make my own claim. I want to claim *him*."

Dedrick took a deep breath and let it out slowly. "Celine, it isn't heard of. A female has never made a claim before."

She smiled at him. "Then let me be the first. There isn't anything saying a female can't claim a male. Help me do this please. It's time, Daddy. It's time for Cole to have his awakening and see that we are perfect for each other."

Again, Dedrick took a deep breath, letting it out slowly. He also brought her back into his arms, hugging her tightly, kissing the top of her head. "Damn you are so much like your mother it's scary."

"Is that a yes?" She held her breath, waiting for the answer.

"Okay, I'll get you your claim. I just hope like hell you know what you're getting yourself into."

Chapter Two

Celine worked on packing her things, a big smile on her face as she did so. On her night stand was the letter, approving her request to claim a male. It has *never* been done before. Ever! Most girls of her kind didn't want to be mated, they wanted to stay free and do as they pleased.

Not Celine.

She wanted Cole. Had since the first time she laid eyes on him, and now she had him. Or sort of. All she had was the claim, now she had to convince him of it. That wasn't going to be easy.

Cole was very prideful. He didn't like handouts, and had this strange sense of honor when it came to the family. Everyone saw it, which was why this whole claiming of him was going to be difficult. She only hoped that when he found out what she did he would be madly in love with her and not mind the how it came about part.

The claim took five months. Five months! That was a hell of a long time to wait this crap out. Drake took Carrick up to his new home alone. In that time Cole and Chase packed up their things, Cole finished his schooling and her father made new arrangements for Chase with his college.

Christmas came, and it was a strange holiday without her grandmother. It was as hard as hell to stay away from Cole, too. Especially when it was showing how much he was suffering from doing the same thing. She saw in his eyes what he wanted and needed. She also saw how damn stubborn he was and how he couldn't look her father in the eye.

When he graduated, her father seemed to make up with him. Celine didn't realize how tense she was over that little fight they had until the tension was off her shoulders with a shake of their hands. She discovered Cole was never going to make his claim on her, which was why she didn't have any guilt over doing it the way she had. After all, the males didn't hold much of a conscious when it came to doing it to a reluctant female.

"I see we dressed for this little event."

Celine smiled, stopped her packing, and turned to her mother. Jaclyn Draeger was still a stunning woman, and Celine noticed right then how much she took after her mother.

Celine had the same delicate figure as she did, same blue eyes, long legs and the 'get what I want' attitude. Often they were mistaken for sisters because of their same dark looks. But with her age Jaclyn began to take inches from her hair, where Celine let her gets longer. It was to her waistline now and she loved it. She had picked up that Cole liked it as well by the way he would stare at it.

"Think it's too much?" she asked Jaclyn with a cock of her head.

She wanted to dress sexy and show enough skin but didn't want to seem like she was showing a too much. It was hot outside, so that was a good excuse to dress like this. She knew it would drive Cole nuts.

Jaclyn held up her hand with her fingers inches apart. "Just a bit."

"I can't help it mom," Celine quickly breathed out, "I'm so excited about seeing him again."

"I know."

"I mean, Daddy got the letter, and then Cole called to tell him they were heading up to Drake's, it's like fate or something." She was rattling on, the words spilling out before she could think. "How perfect could all of this be? I just wish I could have seen his face on the other line when Daddy told him that he wanted Cole to take me along also. That would have been so—" Celine stopped talking when her mother pressed her fingers to her mouth.

"I get it, you're excited about seeing Cole again. I really do," Jaclyn sighed. "But honey, um, what you are wearing isn't going to work if you want to get a man like Cole to grovel at your feet. What you have on is asking to be pounced on," she finished with a short laugh. "Here. Try this."

Jaclyn handed a small gift bag to Celine. She took it and opened it. Inside was a thin summer dress. "Mom!" she gasped, pulling it out.

Jaclyn winked, "Start off slow with him. Now go change."

Celine rushed to the bathroom to change, leaving the door cracked open. "How's Dad taking all of this?"

"Oh, you know him," Jaclyn sang back, "He barks, does some biting, and comes around to my way of thinking. Still wants to kill Cole for being a stubborn ass, but then all I have to do is remind him about how he was when I was chasing after him."

Celine smiled. She loved that story about her parents. How her father refused to have anything to do with a human, but at the same time couldn't keep his hands off of her. It took him almost losing her, a lost child, and her mother just about out the door before he came to his senses and claimed her. It was almost a fairy tale, and would make for an excellent book.

She came out of the bathroom and twirled around. "What'd you think?"

Her mother had given her a simple, yet very sexy pink sundress. The fabric was a pale pink with no decoration on it just tiny pearl buttons going down the middle. It was tight around her breasts, making them appear fuller than they were. There was no way in hell she was going to be able to wear a bra with it. With her dark hair and tan skin, the pink made a perfect showcase for her figure.

"Now that will knock his socks off," Jaclyn pointed her finger at Celine with a smile. But the smile faded quickly and her mother appeared sad.

"Mom?"

"Honey, do you really have any idea as to what you're getting yourself into here? I mean, really understand?"

Celine rolled her eyes and took her clothes to the bags, shoving them inside. "I know about sex, Mom."

"Oh, I know you know about sex," Jaclyn snorted. "With the way you look, your father and I had to make sure you know that, but I mean the other stuff. When Cole finds out about this whole claim thing, and he will find out, are you prepared for what happens? From what I've learned a claim like this never has happened. Your father isn't even sure how strong it is either. Cole could have it easily dissolved."

"You think I'm making a mistake?" Celine felt like her heart was being crushed in her chest.

Jaclyn took her hand and pulled her down to sit on the edge of the bed. "I didn't say that. I'm just saying, with my experience, men like Cole will fight this till the bitter end. Even if there is a strong sexual attraction, and honey he has that. But what I'm saying is be prepared for a big, pretty much hateful rejection. His honor to the family is what keeps him at bay, so keep that in mind."

"I know this isn't going to be easy. I'm not expecting it to be. I just want a chance to show him that it's okay to want something. He wants me, Mom, I see it every time he looks at me. I just need him to act on it."

Jaclyn leaned over and kissed her on the cheek with a smile. "You are so much like your father. So damn stubborn."

"Humph, more like you." Dedrick stood in the doorway, his large frame taking up most of the space. "This is something I could've seen you doing years ago if you had the chance."

Jaclyn leaned back on the bed, arms behind her. Celine watched her mother bat her eyelashes at her father and smile. "I didn't need to do a claiming, wolf boy. I just used the oldest game in the book on your ass. Hot sex."

"Dammit, Jaclyn, is that the kind of shit you want her to do?" he snapped.

Yep, her father was still pissed over this whole thing.

"Dedrick," Jaclyn sighed, standing up. "As much as I hate to admit it, she's not a little girl anymore. We've talked about this."

"It doesn't mean I want her to go have sex all over the place!" he yelled.

"I'm going to go downstairs and let you two talk," Celine said, quickly slipping from her room to go downstairs.

"They still at it?"

Celine jumped. Uncle Stefan was coming out from the dining room, a picnic basket in hand.

"Yep."

He smiled, shaking his head, "Your father doesn't want to let you go. You're his miracle, Celine. You and your mother."

"I know." She lowered her head, only to have him raise it up with a finger under her chin.

"The heart wants what it wants. We all understand that. Just don't let him lose his little girl and I think your old man will be just fine," he smiled, then took a deep breath. "Damn he's going to be a bear to live with for a few days."

Stefan shook his head, putting the basket down next to the bags in front of the door. He went up the stairs and she headed to the back.

* * * *

"So how long are you going to be a grumpy bastard?" Chase asked Cole.

"I'm not a grumpy bastard," Cole said.

"Then what would you call it?" Chase crossed his arms over his chest in the passenger seat of Cole's jeep. A jeep that Dedrick and the rest of the family bought him for graduation. "Ever since you got that letter and then the call from Dedrick about Celine going up to Drake's with us, you've been this," he indicated with his hand towards Cole. "One big ass grumpy bastard."

Chase knew something was up, but he just couldn't put his finger on it. For years, now, he knew, just like the family, that Cole had a thing for Celine. It was written all over his face. But what had Chase having fun with Cole, was the simple fact that his damn brother was too stubborn to do anything about it. Chase knew for a fact if he was in Cole's shoes he would've put a claim on her years ago just so no other could. Celine was damn hot!

"We could've been up there by now if we didn't have to stop and pick her up," Cole grumbled again.

It was another thing he started that Chase noticed. All the grumbling. Cole was constantly in a bad mood.

"Come on, Celine is fun!" Chase said. "She's like one of the boys. You'll never know she's in the back seat."

"Yeah right." They turned into the drive and sped down to the house. Cole skidded to a stop in front of the door. "She isn't one of the boys," he turned in his seat to Chase. "And if you look at the shit on the porch, you'll see she's all girl with a shitload of girly crap!"

"Cole, you need to get laid." Chase slapped him on the shoulder before opening the door and getting out before his brother could hit him. "You're a crab ass."

"Crab ass!" Cole got out and rushed around the front of the jeep, making Chase run to the back. "Where the hell are we going to put all that shit?"

"In the trailer that you're going to hook up," Stefan answered.

"Stefan!" Chase smiled big, mostly because he was saved from being killed by his brother. "How the hell are you?"

Stefan laughed, "Better than you it seems." He shook hands with Chase before handing him the picnic basket in his hand. "Here. Sid fixed you all some lunch for the trip and I'm instructed to get the bags on the porch. Think there are more upstairs, and I know that Sid is sending you two with some shit for Drake."

"Please tell me that Jaclyn put some of her cinnamon rolls in here," Chase mumbled.

"Just minus one," Stefan mumbled back. "How's it going, Cole?"

Chase took a quick glance into the basket before putting it in the back seat. "Oh, Cole's in a mood."

"I'm going to show you mood!" Cole lunged at Chase, who quickly got out of the way.

Chase couldn't keep himself from laughing at his brother, but when Cole stopped chasing him and stood still as a statue all joking disappeared. He turned to see what had grabbed his brother's attention, knowing before he saw it what it was.

Celine.

She was standing on the porch, bag in hand dressed in a tight little pink dress that even had Chase forgetting that she had eyes only for his brother. She was breath taking and for the first time in years, Chase had to agree with Cole. She was *definitely* not one of the boys.

He kept staring at her while he moved up behind Cole. "Yep. Temptation itself, standing there. You are so screwed," he said softly behind Cole.

Cole elbowed him, knocking the wind from him.

Stefan whistled, "Come on boys. Time's wasting."

Chase grabbed Cole's arm to drag him away. They pulled the jeep to the back, hooked up the trailer, then went back to the front where Dedrick and Stefan both started to load it up with furniture. Drake had called and asked if he could have his bedroom furniture. But it wasn't only his room that got loaded up.

"What are you guys doing? Packing the whole house up?" Cole grunted while he helped to load up a third bed."

"Drake has a four bedroom home and no beds but one," Stefan was grunting with the weight of a bed. Behind them, Chase was helping Dedrick with a dresser. "Would you like to sleep on the floor?"

They got to the house around ten, but it was after twelve before the three were on the road. Cole sat in the jeep while Celine said good-bye to her family. Chase pulled Stefan off to the side to have a word with him, and hoped he could get some information on what was going on.

"You want to let me in here?" Chase asked Stefan.

Stefan frowned and crossed his arms over his chest, "What'd you mean?"

"Something's going on Stefan. I can see it, and Cole has not been himself for a couple of weeks now." Chase scratched the side of his face, glanced at the jeep before lowering his voice and going on. "He got this letter and ever since has been one big ass crab to live with. You know anything about it?"

Stefan rubbed his chin, head down like he was thinking about something. He rubbed the back of his neck before looking back up at Chase. "Dammit, he knows."

"Knows what?"

"They weren't supposed to inform him for a few weeks. Shit!"

"Stefan?"

"Dedrick, come here!"

Now Chase was really confused. He stood still, almost holding his breath.

"What's wrong?" Dedrick asked.

"Cole got the letter early." Stefan said.

Dedrick's face seemed to darken. Pissed off seemed too mild from what Chase was witnessing on Dedrick's face.

"Those dumb fuckers!" Dedrick growled.

"We can't let her go now," Stefan sighed.

"Wait a minute." Chase held up his hand, getting both of their attentions. "What is so important about that letter?"

Dedrick looked from him to Stefan, who only shrugged. "Celine knows Cole is her mate," Dedrick told Chase.

Chase also shrugged, "Yeah, so do I and the rest of the family. So?"

"She petitioned the Cabinet for a claim on Cole," Stefan added.

Both brows went up and Chase couldn't stop his mouth from opening in shock over what he heard. "What?" he gasped, "Females don't—"

"We know," Stefan and Dedrick both said at the same time.

"And they approved of it?" Chase asked.

"Sort of," Stefan answered. "They are granting her a time frame to get Cole to make the claim on *her*. Females can't make claims, but they know that she is Cole's mate. She has the summer to convince him and if he doesn't then she is free for another to come along and make a claim on her."

"And he knows all of this?" Chase thumbed in the direction of Cole.

"If he got the letter he does," Dedrick said.

Chase couldn't help himself. He began to laugh. Both Stefan and Dedrick frowned at him like he'd lost his mind. When Stefan gave Dedrick a questioning look, Chase shook his head and held up his hands. He tried to get himself under control, but it was too damn hard.

Now everything made sense. Cole's dark mood, the way he avoided being around Celine or talking about her. This trip—everything! Cole was pissed that his mate took things out of his hands and was forcing him. Well hell, if he wasn't so honorable then it would be him making the claim, forcing her.

"I'm sorry," Chase said, holding up one hand and wiping the tears with the other. "But that just explains so much right now."

"Like?" Dedrick asked.

"His mood," Chase sniffed, and quickly rubbed his face, trying to get serious. "Since that letter came he has been a real bear to live with. From what Natasha told us, kind of like you," he pointed at Dedrick. "So I guess Celine *is* a lot like her mother, huh?"

"Not helping there, Chase," Stefan put his arm around Chase's shoulder, pushing him away from Dedrick. "Come on."

Chase sobered up the closer they got to the jeep, "Listen, Stefan, you may be right." His eyes landed on Celine. "Maybe it isn't a good idea to let her go with us. It all could backfire on her. I don't want to see her get her heart broken."

"Which is why I'm going to tell you to keep an eye on things." They stopped next to the trailer. "Everyone needs someone to talk to. Fill Drake in on what's going on and he'll help out with Cole. The man's stubborn, we all know it. But he also has Celine on his ass, so he really doesn't stand a chance," he shrugged.

"How bad was Jaclyn really?"

Stefan smiled big, "Relentless."

"Can we go now?" Cole snapped as he came around the trailer. "This drive is like six hours at least."

"I call shotgun!" Celine yelled, kissing Jaclyn then Dedrick quickly before running to the passenger side of the jeep.

Chase took a deep breath, letting it out loudly, "Yep. This is definitely going to be interesting."

* * * *

Cole drove as fast as he dared with the trailer of furniture behind him. He had one hell of a time keeping his eyes on the road and not on the mouth-watering legs in the seat next to him.

Celine wasn't supposed to be sitting in front. Chase was. And Since Chase thought all this shit was so funny, he wasn't at all surprised that he was willing to let Celine sit in front. Thank God he had his sunglasses on. If either knew how many times he was glancing over at her legs, he wouldn't be able to live it down.

"Anyone care for a sandwich?" Chase asked from the back.

Cole took a deep breath, once more tore his eyes from her legs, to focus back on the road.

"Don't you want to stop somewhere to eat them?" Celine asked, turning in the seat.

The move had him glancing at her and his eyes went from her legs right up to her breasts. The top outline made his mouth water and caused his damn dick to stir in his pants. Fuck he needed to get laid, but he'd be damned if it was going to be with Celine. Cole's jaw reminded him of what her father would do if he put his hands on her, but then that damn letter he got was strange.

Dear Mr. Sexton.

This letter is to inform you of a claim that has been placed towards you. Celine Draeger has petitioned the Cabinet to recognize you as her mate. Of course, we cannot do this but what we are able to do at this time is put a hold on her for three months. In that time, no other male will be able to request a claim on her. You have three months to make your claim.

Now how the hell did she do that? Females couldn't put claim on, only males could. And from the way Dedrick socked him, he didn't think there was a chance, if he wanted to, that it was going to happen.

"We really need to get there, Celine," Cole sighed, forcing himself to keep his eyes on the road and not look at her. "It's already going to be dark by the time we reach the town, and then I still have to find Drake's place."

"Fine," she shrugged, her breasts rising, so was his damn dick. "We can eat in the jeep. No big deal to me." She reached to the back and he took another glance at her.

Damn that fucking dress was tight!

"Well if you see a rest stop," Chase added, "At least pull in there. Don't feel like pissing on the side of the road."

"Chase!" Cole snapped.

Celine giggled.

"Sorry." Chase mumbled.

"So," Celine bounced back in her seat, halfway turned towards him. "What'cha been up to so far this summer?"

Cole rotated his neck, trying to release the tension from his shoulders. "Helping Adrian get settled into their house."

"How does Aunt Skyler like the place?"

"Loves the space," Chase put in.

"Guess they outgrew the other house," Cole said. "The boys are very happy to have their own rooms. I helped Adrian fix up the attic for Alex, so they were all very happy."

"Yeah, that's right, you went into carpentry," she pointed at him. "Any ideas yet on what you're going to have your place look like?"

You can have a normal conversation with her. Just don't let on that you know about the letter. You don't touch her, then everything goes back the way it was at the end of the summer. "No not yet. Thought I might see what Drake's place looks like to get a few cabin ideas first."

"Good idea. I can help also." He looked her right in the face and she rolled her eyes. "Mom says I've got a good eye for that kind of stuff."

He didn't say anything about it, just gave his attention back to the road. She ate a sandwich, chatted with Chase and he drove on with a throbbing dick that refused to go down. When he saw the sign for a rest stop, Cole took the turn.

"Thought we weren't going to stop," Chase smarted off.

"I'm getting a cramp and need to walk it off," Cole told him. "So if you two want to stretch, go for it." He parked and got out before either could say a word to him.

Cole rushed to the bathroom, glad that there wasn't anyone inside it.

Shifters 5: Cole's Awakening

In a stall, behind a locked door, he was finally able to breathe right. He took several deep breaths, trying to get himself under control.

"Fuck me this is going to be a long ass trip," he said to himself.

He leaned against the wall, right over the toilet. This wasn't fair, he thought. He should be relaxed and enjoying the move. It took him months to accept the fact that Natasha was still going to take care of him. She'd left him and Chase the property for a good reason, so there was no point in fighting it. That was the point Adrian had made to him one night.

One good long talk with Adrian and Cole was seeing things differently. At least where the property and what Natasha had left them was concerned. She'd made sure both of them had the funds to build a house. In fact, Natasha shocked the whole family with how much money she had put up. And what she gave Cole and Chase assured them both that they wouldn't have to work if they didn't want to.

She owned a marina in Cape Cod, as well as a few other small businesses in the town and the city. It seemed that her husband was a genius and Natasha was just as smart. But she sold a few of them, leaving three that would make the most money and leaving them to her three children.

It was hard for Cole to admit that he was part of the family and take the gift that was given him, but he did. The only thing he knew without a doubt, he wasn't going to take Celine.

Cole leaned one arm against the wall. He unbuckled his belt, pulled the snap on his jeans, and pushed the zipper down. Closing his eyes, he reached inside, bringing his cock out.

Damn he was hard—painfully so in fact.

Cole didn't plan on doing anything more than putting some space between him and her long enough to get his senses under control. So far that plan wasn't working.

He started off slow, just a simple stroke of his cock to ease some of the pain, but before long he was moving his hand fast and holding it tight. He pumped, hissing softly at the pleasure, which went down his spine and quickly formed in the tight sac between his legs. His balls tightened up and with his mouth open in a silent moan he came, aiming for the toilet.

"Shit," he sighed when his climax was over, breathing a bit faster. It wasn't what he wanted, but it was going to have to do for the moment.

He fixed himself, flushed and went out to wash his hands. When he was finished, Chase walked into the bathroom.

"I was wondering what happened to you."

Cole dried his hands on a towel and tossed it into the trash. "Took a walk around. Felt like I was getting a cramp. And in case you want to know the rest of the details, I took a piss. No, I didn't have to shit at this time."

"Jesus, Cole, I was just wondering."

Cole rubbed his face then the back of his neck, "Sorry. I'm just on edge."

Chase went over to one of the urinals. "She's gotten even prettier since the last time we saw her, so I can see why."

Cole frowned at his back, not liking what he was hearing. "What?"

"Come on Cole, don't act like you haven't noticed," Chase finished, flushed and went over to the sink, washing his own hands. "I've seen you glancing at her since we left the house." He also tossed the towel he used into the trash. "Hey, you think I might have a chance with her?" he asked with a slight hit to Cole's chest.

Before Cole could answer it, Chase left the bathroom. Cole came out of his daze quickly to go after him.

"Chase!" he yelled.

But he didn't get to say any more. Chase met up with Celine and quickly put his arm around her shoulders. Cole didn't even realize he was doing a low growl until it left his lips.

"Let's get going." He didn't mean for it to come out sounding harsh or like he was in a bad mood, but something about his brother touching her bothered him.

They drove for another couple of hours before stopping again, this time for gas. Everything in the basket was gone, so while Cole pumped the gas, Celine and Chase got more snacks.

At six in the evening, they reached the town and all three were starving. But Cole didn't want to have to sit in a restaurant for dinner. He knew he couldn't handle having Chase sit next to her flirting and he sure as hell didn't trust himself to sit next to her.

So listening to them complain, Cole kept on driving. He followed the directions Drake gave him, but the darker it became the harder it was to find the markers Drake told him to look for. Drake said it would only take twenty minutes from town to the road that went up to the drive. After forty-five minutes he pulled over to the side of the road in frustration.

"I don't know where the hell I'm supposed to go," he sighed, rubbing his face. He was tired and hungry. And no shit, what a surprise. Horny!

Celine looked around then pointed behind them, "Wasn't there a road back there?"

"Could be," Cole shrugged.

"Give me the map." Chase moved his fingers in front of Cole until he handed over the directions and the map. While he was reading it over, Cole turned to Celine.

"Tired?"

"Some," she smiled. "Dying to see Drake's place. He called me last week to tell me that Carrick has it all set up." She leaned to the side, resting her head on the seat. "She loves it up here. Said it was the first time she was ever in a place that felt like home and not a prison. The woods are great, and there are many places to swim. He said he found a small cabin in the woods and started working on it—was hoping you would help with it."

"Okay, got it," Chase called out. "That side road we passed about half a mile back is the one we need to turn off on."

Cole tore his eyes from Celine. "Okay. Drake is going to have to put a marker there or something. The rest of the family is going to get lost trying to find it too." He put the jeep in gear and made a U-turn to go back the way they had come.

He found the road, turned and held on for a bumpy ride. It was a long dirt road that curved towards the left. Chase pointed out that there was another over grown road to the right, but Cole was following the one that seemed used.

The woods were beautiful. Natasha had picked the perfect place for them to have a home built. Any shifter would love to have something like this. The freedom to be what and who they are.

They came out in a clearing that had all three of them breathless. Drake's home was amazing. It was a standard two-story log cabin home, only it didn't look so standard. It was big. Four large windows were on both levels, a wooden wraparound porch and plants all over the place. It definitely was a nice home.

"Now I'm impressed." Cole went around the circle drive to park right in front of the door. He got out slowly, staring up at the place where he was going to be staying until he got his own home built.

"I was wondering if you guys were ever going to get here," Drake came out of a shed off to the right of the house.

"Drake!" Celine quickly got out of the jeep and ran to him.

Drake caught her, hugging her tight. Cole narrowed his eyes on the two, wondering what it would be like if she ran to him like that. Would he hold her that tight?

"There's that look again," Chase sang in his ear.

Cole elbowed him in the gut. "Knock it off."

"Well don't stand there you two." Carrick crossed her arms over her chest, leaning against the open door. "Dinner is waiting."

"Now that is what I was dying to hear!" Chase smiled, rubbing his hands together.

Cole took a step towards the front door but stopped when he heard Celine laugh. He looked at them. She was still in Drake's arms, both smiling.

"Cole, come on!" Carrick called out to him. "Before those two get their hands on it."

He nodded at her, glanced once more at Celine then shoved his hands into his pockets and walked inside the house.

Chapter Three

"So you ready to get that stuff unloaded?" Drake asked Cole after they finished their meal. He handed a beer to Cole, then one to Chase. "I mean, unless you want to sleep on the floor."

"I'll help if it guarantees me not having to sleep on the floor," Celine raised her hand with a smile.

They were sitting at a round table in the kitchen. Carrick had fixed a large meal and they ate every bit of it. Celine had to fight with Drake over the last steak, which Carrick ended up cutting in half. She was full and tired. But there was a ton of stuff needing to be unpacked.

"Okay you guys do your thing, and I'll clean up," Carrick said, pushing away from the table. "Celine gets the room next to us, bathroom is next and then the last two rooms Cole and Chase can decide who gets which room."

Celine pushed away from the table and went up to Drake. "Why do I have the room next to yours?" she whispered. "I don't want to hear you two at night."

Drake took hold of her shoulders, turned her and pushed her out of the kitchen. The front room was large with a rock fireplace built into a side wall that hid the stairs. There was two leather sofas placed back to back, one facing the fireplace and the other a television. The television was built into the wall, built in shelves around it, two leather chairs, wooden end tables and lamps completed the furnishings in the room.

Drake kept walking Celine until they were outside, but he didn't stop next to the jeep. No, he kept pushing till they were back at the shed.

"Okay, CeeCee, give," he sighed.

She turned, frowning. "What're you talking about?"

"Oh you know," he wagged his finger at her. "Don't play that innocent crap with me. I know you better than he does. Hell I wouldn't be surprised if even better than your father. Who I might add has called twice now ranting about shit I only know half of. So spill it. What game are you playing now?"

She crossed her arms over her chest, narrowing her eyes at him. "I'm not playing any game, Drake. How could you—"

He silenced her with his hand over her mouth. "Dad did call me to tell me what you tried to do. So be very careful what you say, little girl."

She thought about it for a few moments. If Uncle Stefan called Drake, then he knew everything, not just parts of it. Knowing Drake as she did, it wouldn't take too long before he figured it *all* out.

She took a step back, kept narrowing her eyes on him with both hands on her hips, foot tapping. "What do you know?"

Drake chuckled, shaking his head. "Oh no, you first."

She took a deep breath, letting it out slowly. "I know he's my mate."

"And?"

Celine rolled her eyes, "Come on, Drake, you know the rest."

"But I want to hear it. I want to hear from your own lips what you tried to do," the left side of his lips twitching up into a grin. "Because I'm having a very hard time believing that you really did try this shit."

"No."

"No?" he cocked his head to the side.

"That's right. No. No I'm not going to tell you what you already know."

"Ohhh," he chuckled without humor. "Girl, you are playing with major fire here!" It sounded like he wanted to yell at her but was working hard to keep his voice down. "What the hell made you think that you could put a claim on him?"

"Why not?" she charged back. "What makes it all right for you guys to do it and not us?"

"Come on, CeeCee!" he groaned. Both hands fisted into his hair. Drake walked around in a circle before stopping in front of her, one hand on his hip the other wagging a finger in her face. He opened his mouth several times, nothing came out. Again, he ran his hands in his hair and paced in a circle.

"Don't you think you are blowing all of this way out of proportion?" she sighed.

"No I'm not!" he snapped, stopping again in front of her. "Celine this is serious shit here."

Again, she crossed her arms over her chest and leaned to the side, "Why? Because a female did it or because it's me?"

"There's no difference."

"The hell there is!" Now he was raising his voice. "You know how damn prideful he is. Do you think he is going to go along with this shit?"

"He doesn't know?"

"Are you sure?"

The question had her pausing. Did he know? Did they tell him that she tried to put a claim on him? Damn, she hoped like hell they didn't. If Cole knew then that would fuck up all of her plans.

"You don't know, do you?" he asked. "You have no clue if Cole is aware of what you tried."

"What did you want me to do, wait around until *he* decides?" She emphasized what she was saying by pointing back towards the house. "If I wait around until he gets his shit together then someone else is going to claim me. We both know that." She moved her hand back and forth between him and her. Drake rubbed his face and she grabbed hold of his arms, getting his full attention. "Drake I need him. Don't you understand that?"

Drake took a deep breath before pulling her into his arms, hugging her tight, resting his chin on the top of her head. "I understand CeeCee," he sighed. "But this way is wrong. I don't have a good feeling about it. You could get seriously hurt here."

"I know, Drake, but I also have to try. It's the only way to get him to do what he needs to do."

"Hey, you two going to give us a hand?" Chase yelled from the trailer.

Celine looked over at Chase, but her eyes landed on Cole. She watched his every move as she rested her head on Drake's chest.

Everything about him was what she hungered for. His thick arms, holding her at night, the wide expanse of his chest for her head to rest upon. She wanted to touch the muscles under the shirt. Feel the twitching of his skin when her fingers touched him. She hungered to smell his desire for her. To taste his flesh and hear his moans of pleasure when she took him into her mouth and body. God, just thinking about it had her wet and throbbing. Something she was pretty sure Drake could pick up on by the way he tightened his hold on her.

"So what's your plan of action?" Drake sounded defeated.

Celine kept staring at Cole. She couldn't help herself, not when he was helping Chase pick up a dresser and the muscles on his arms bulged tight in the sleeve of his shirt.

"I don't know," she sighed against his chest, fisting her hands in Drake's shirt.

"Well you better come up with one fast." He patted her on the back then pulled out of the embrace. "And it better be a damn good one."

Drake kissed her cheek before leaving her there to help bring the furniture inside. Celine hugged herself, thinking about what she was going to do. The only thing that came to mind was the story of her parents. Jaclyn pursued Dedrick relentlessly. She was everywhere Dedrick was, tempting him with what he wanted but was too afraid to take. Maybe that was the same thing Celine needed to do. Maybe she needed to be everywhere that Cole was, tempting him to do the right thing and claim her. It was the only plan she could think of.

Celine helped with the bags while the guys brought the furniture inside. Once the first bed was brought in, Carrick and Chase began to set them up. Celine went behind them to make up the beds. She also put Chase and Cole's bags in their rooms.

It was after midnight by the time she was able to go into Cole's room at the end of the hall to make up the bed. Cole was in the bathroom, taking a shower, Chase downstairs taking his. There were three bathrooms in the house; one was Drake and Carrick's attached to their bedroom. She dropped the sheets and blankets on top of the mattress and went to work. It was the last bed to be made up and then she was going to crawl into her own.

"What're you doing in here?"

Celine jumped and turned around quickly. Cole was standing in the doorway, towel only around his waist, hair wet and stuck to his face and neck.

"Dammit, Cole you scared me," she gasped, turning back around to finish what she was doing. On purpose, she made sure her ass was in his line of vision and even did a bit of swaying. "What's it look like I'm doing?"

"Invading my space," he grumbled.

She smiled, even though he couldn't see it. "You and Chase brought all the stuff in, thought it was the least I could do to make sure you guys didn't have to worry about making up the beds." She walked around to the other side and bent over it, smoothing out all the wrinkles. When she glanced up, she saw that his eyes were down her dress. Perfect! "There you go." She slapped her hands on the bed, straightened up and walked over to him. "You should sleep like a baby."

"Is that so?"

"Sure." She smiled. "There isn't any reason why you shouldn't." She made to go past him and leave, but he stopped her without warning when his arm came out to the other side of the doorway, blocking her. Slowly she turned her head to look at him, one eyebrow going up in question.

"I'm too old for games, Celine. So please don't play any with me."

"I'm not playing games, Cole." She tried to put on her best smile and sweetest voice. She pushed his arm away and stepped out in the hall. "All I've done is make your bed. Night."

Celine went all the way back to her room, smiling. Yep, he was affected, just like she remembered.

* * * *

Josh Stan stood in his new lab looking over the two specimens in their cages. He didn't look upon them as people, only animals, created by his good friend, Conner Martin, for the sole purpose of testing. Nothing more. They were the means of wiping out the infected; it was that, plain and simple. They were here only so he could find a way to kill them off.

"He broke another set of chains. The last dose of drugs wore off faster than the others."

Josh turned and followed his assistant, Jason Spencer, down the stairs to the two large cages that held his pets. Kane was his name, a name he'd given himself just like he named the other one. He was chained down tight on his cot, drugged heavily so he couldn't move and drugged so he had a nice size erection, which had diminished now. Kane moved his head as much as he could when Josh walked up to him. Hate burned brightly in his red eyes.

"He tried to grab at one of the guys who touched Sasha's hair," Jason told him.

Josh looked over at Sasha, a small blonde girl who was completely useless. She was curled up in a ball on her cot, looking scared. Twins. That was what they were supposed to be. The egg split, and Martin put one back in the freezer until later. He'd never thought it was possible for one to get all the animal traits and the other nothing when the egg split or that one would be female and the other male. They should be fraternal twins, but they were identical, something that wasn't possible ever, yet he was looking at it right now. Identical twins, male/female—human/shifter.

How the hell was anything like this possible? It should be one or the other, not both! Hell, they didn't look one damn bit alike. Kane was dark, with a large build. He had sandy brown hair with a few black streaks and was strong enough to kill anything. Sasha was petite, blonde, and useless. She had no shifter traits.

But she did have her uses, even if they were small. She kept Kane under control. If she didn't, Josh would have gotten rid of her a long time ago. He hated keeping things that were useless.

"Keep acting up. Keep pissing me off and I'll give her to one of the guards," Josh told him. "And you'll watch the whole thing." He pointed a finger at him. "Hear her screams."

Kane strained against his chains, growling deeply.

Jason walked up with his usual cruel smile in place. Josh knew that he loved walking around Kane's cage, telling the animal all the things he would love to do to his sister. Taunting him until he did something—which would cost him some kind of punishment. That was one of Jason's favorite things to do, punish Kane and he was damn good at it.

"The last dose only lasted twelve hours," Jason told him. "We need it to last at least twenty-four."

"Are we ready to test the breeding again?" Josh asked.

"Yeah. We snatched a couple of girls from the streets. With a few drops of that stuff you made they were no problem."

Josh motioned with his hand for the others to pull the chains on Kane. His large arms went over his head, and his legs spread out. The cage door opened, and Josh himself walked in. He held a syringe in his hand with enough drugs to make Kane stay hard for hours. Josh needed to know what made those bastards breed. He wanted to know how to prevent them from touching another innocent girl. He jabbed the needle in the thick leg and within seconds, Kane was hard and ready. Almost ten inches of cock stood straight up.

"Let's get started," Josh said.

Two guards helped a young girl walk into the lab room. She was stripped and cleaned. She'd also been given a drug to arouse her. The guards walked her into the cage, and then helped her to straddle Kane. Within seconds, they were all watching and waiting.

"You better come this time," Josh warned, snapping his fingers. A guard brought Sasha over and Josh took hold of her arm, yanking her over so she could watch the scene of her brother's rape. "Or else."

Kane glared and yelled, bringing the show to an end. The girl on top of Kane also screamed. Her whole body shook before falling down on top of him. He stared up at the ceiling saying nothing.

"Good. Now bring in the other one." Josh turned his back on him, taking Sasha back to her own cage. "You have a long night ahead of you, Kane. Hope you enjoy it."

* * * *

"Breakfast!"

Cole jolted away, or more like jumped and twisted out of bed so fast he fell right out. He'd slept hard, something he hadn't done in years. With a groan, he dropped his face down on the side of the bed. He was still tired and aw shit, what a surprise. Hard as hell.

"Knock-knock." Cole turned his head toward Carrick's voice. The door opened and her head came around. "Shit, you fall out of bed?"

'Only when you yelled," he answered, refusing to move for fear she would see his hard-on.

"Oh, sorry about that," she laughed. "Drake is usually out doing something and I have to yell to let him know when the food is ready. You're the last one to get up and I figured you might want to eat while it's hot and before Celine and Drake get their hands on it. I swear I don't know where that girl puts it."

"So where is the bucket of sunshine?"

Carrick came into his room and went right to the window. While she had her back to him, Cole got up off the floor and quickly covered up with the sheet.

"Chase got up early and wanted to go over to look at the property, and Drake took Celine into the woods to show her around. With what they snuck out of the house, I'm going to take a guess and say they went for a swim." She turned around and smiled, leaning back against the window frame, hands behind her. "So you and I get to eat alone and talk," she shrugged. "If you want."

"Can I do it with clothes on?"

Carrick lowered her head and nodded. "Sorry." She pushed away from the window, heading back to the door. "I'll see you downstairs when you're ready."

The door closed and he dropped back face down on the bed with a groan. Lust was a bitch and painful.

Cole dressed and went down stairs. The smell of bacon and eggs had his mouth watering. When he walked into the kitchen, Carrick handed him a plate, loaded. He sat down and dug in

"So how does this honor thing work with you guys?" Carrick asked.

Cole stopped chewing to look up at her. His mouth was full, but he knew what she was asking. He licked his lips, sat back and wiped his mouth while he finished chewing.

"Just ask what you want to ask," he said.

"Are you going to claim her?"

That was what Cole liked about Carrick. She came right to the point. "No."

"No?" One eye brow went up. "And how do you figure that's going to work?"

Cole picked up a piece of bacon and took a bite. "Why do you care?"

"Okay." Both hands went up and she sat back in her chair, crossing one leg over the other. "Look I might not know all the ins and outs of your guys, but I do know a bit about her." She thumbed towards the back door. "Remember I did live in the same house with her for a while. She's used to getting what she wants and Cole old buddy I see her sights set on you." She pointed at him.

"So."

"So!"

"Carrick, Celine isn't going to get her way this time. I have a bit more control than what I think you're giving me credit for."

"Uh-huh."

"Don't believe me?"

She shook her head and chuckled. "Not with the way you've been looking at her. Just a matter of time little boy before she gets so far under your skin you won't be able to breathe without her."

"Thanks for the vote of confidence."

"I call it like I see it." She took a drink of her coffee and smiled at him. "Boy you are so screwed, especially if Drake helps her out. You won't stand a chance. I've seen it all first hand, sweetie."

He shook his head and stood up, taking his plate with him to the sink. "I think I'm going to walk around and check the place out. All this talking could upset my breakfast." She laughed and he stopped to give her a quick kiss on the cheek. "But it was very good. Thanks."

Cole left out the back door. Hands in his pockets he headed for the woods. The outdoors smelled great and the woods were perfect. It felt like real freedom to be walking through brush, making your own trail. Cole never knew how caged he felt until he was walking in the woods. He came across a little cabin that appeared as if someone had been working on the porch. Cole stopped to study the little place and shook his head. It could be so perfect if fixed up. From the angle he was standing, he saw it needed a new roof, and he would bet major work on the inside.

He walked over to it, stepping up onto the porch. When he peeked inside his breath caught in his chest and his body came alive. Celine was inside, all the way in the back, changing her clothes.

Yes, he could see the place needed work. Whoever had designed this cabin, the space had been laid out to allow the front room to be separated into more than one room with a bedroom in the back. Cole should have been looking at the structure but his eyes were locked on Celine. She had her back to the door, a towel wrapped around her body, another on top of her head. She was squirming and he had to bite his lower lip when he saw the bottoms of a bikini slip down her legs to the floor. Another twist of her body and she was dropping the top with it. Just knowing that she was naked under that towel had his cock pounding.

She bent over, dug in a bag that he didn't even see on the floor, and took out a tank top. The towel on her head came off, the one around her body dropped and Cole thought he was going to come in his jeans. The short, tight shirt went over her head, then she bent over again, pulling out some short shorts and she stepped into them as well. Just seeing her bare backside was pure torture. It was a sight that would forever be burned into his memory.

When the shorts were over her ass, he made a sound to let her know he was there. She jumped and turned around. Her face flushed a bit, but it didn't seem to stop the smile from spreading over her face.

"Cole! What are you doing here?"

She quickly buttoned and zipped up the shorts while he strolled inside in a lazy manner. He couldn't let her see how badly she affected him. If she only knew how hard he got at times then she would use it against him to get what she wanted. He had to keep telling himself that.

"Checking out the woods." He stopped in the archway to what he thought was the bedroom, put both hands up over his head and leaned forwards slightly. "What about you? Changing clothes?"

"Oh that." She looked down at the suit, her smile still on her face. "Went swimming with Drake. He's going to take Chase to town and I thought I'd go with them. So I was changing."

Cole watched her every move. His eyes landed on the necklace around her neck. Without thinking, he reached out and picked it up. "You still wear it."

"I love it."

He looked her in the eye, dropping the necklace, moving his hand to her throat. He rubbed a vein that was pounding quickly under his thumb. Thinking went right out the door for him. Keeping his hand around her throat, Cole moved her to the back, pressing her up against the wall. His eyes were locked with hers, the throbbing in the vein matched his cock's throbbing.

It felt like a dream. One that he couldn't seem to wake up from before he did something very stupid. His head lowered and before he could stop himself he was pressing his lips to hers.

Celine opened to him and Cole dived in. He plunged his tongue into her mouth and she closed around it, sucking it hard, intensifying the pounding of his cock.

He deepened the kiss, slanting his head to the side. Both hands went down to her chest, cupping them, squeezing her breasts with a moan before going further to the button of her jean shorts. With a yank he had them open enough to have his hands inside, cupping his hands over them, holding her close by the grip.

Celine shocked him even more by cupping him between the legs. He didn't stop her when she pulled on his belt, opened his own jeans up and closed her hand around the base of his shaft.

He was hard, so painfully hard and her hand, trying to go around him was enough to drive him insane with pent up lust! She stroked him and it weakened his knees to a point he thought he was going to drop to the ground.

It was going too fast. This was not what he had intended to do today. Kissing her was a no-no, but fuck if her hand around his damn dick, moving up and down, didn't feel like heaven.

"Shit, we have to stop," he moaned the second he broke the kiss and removed his hands from her shorts. "It was a mistake to kiss you."

"I'm not ready to stop.'

Cole watched her with hooded eyes as she went down to her knees before him. He held his breath, watching her tug on his jeans until she had the whole length of his cock out in front of her.

One hand was around the base, and the other she pushed back into his jeans, cupping his balls. Cole growled low at the pleasure. He was also breathing hard from the anticipation of what she was going to do, having a pretty damn good idea what it was.

Her mouth opened, and he watched long enough to see her take the head into her mouth and then he closed his eyes and tossed his head back. She sucked half into her mouth, teased the underside with her tongue, and Cole loved every damn motherfucking second of it.

How many wet dreams had he had over the years of her doing this? Too damn many. How many times did he jack off in the shower, wishing it was her hand? Every fucking night. Was this right now? Hell no! But it sure did feel fucking great!

Cole opened his eyes and looked down, watching her suck him in and out. The pressure she put on it, the pull and the way her hands teased his balls had him knowing that this was going to be a short ride. He was going to come real soon and had no intentions of holding it back.

When she started to tease the entrance of his ass with a finger, Cole started to fuck her face. He leaned against her, hands over the nearby window frame to hold himself off. He panted with each stroke inside her mouth, feeling his climax coming fast and faster. She moaned against him and he hissed.

How could he let this happen? How could he just let her go down on her knees, take his damn dick out, and blow him like this? He didn't have the answer to it, and at the moment he didn't give a shit about it. All he cared about was feeling his release from her hands and lips.

"Shit, I'm going to come," he groaned, closing his eyes, pumping faster and shorter.

That finger that teased his ass went in, and Cole lost it. He tensed up, even went up on his toes right before he exploded into her mouth. He couldn't yell, couldn't moan, couldn't make a sound to save his life, it felt that good.

Spurt after spurt seemed to shoot out of him, and like the greedy little girl she could be, Celine drank every drop he had. He did cry out when she wiggled her finger in his ass and somehow took his whole dick down her throat.

"CeeCee!"

Like cold water, Drake's voice snapped him right out of his trance. Cole opened his eyes and stared out the window. He saw Drake coming toward the cabin, through the brush.

Breathing hard, he pushed away from her. He backed up all the way to the other side of the room, trying to put his dick back in his pants before Drake came in.

"Dammit, Celine!" he snapped as quietly as he could. "What the fuck was that?"

"You know what that was." She stood up, also fixing her shorts. "And from what I tasted you enjoyed it also."

"God dammit!" He finished with his jeans to rub his face then ran a trembling hand through his hair. "That should *never* have happened."

"Then why'd you let me," she tossed back, then after cleaning off her mouth with a towel, she quickly began shoving the towels and her bathing suit in the bag.

"CeeCee, you ready?" Drake yelled.

She stood up and Cole quickly grabbed hold of her arm, "This never happened, Celine. You understand."

The hurt he saw in her eyes tore at his gut. But shit! He couldn't have her just going down on him when he was in a weakened state, which was whenever he looked at her!

"The kiss, or the blow job?" she smarted off, jerking her arm from his hold. "I'm coming, Drake!"

Cole kept his mouth shut while she tore from the cabin, like hell was on her ass. And boy what an ass. Not five minutes ago, he had his hands on it. She was so hot he could probably have taken her right there on the floor. But what does he do? He let her go down on him without a single 'no'. He went back over to the window, watching her leave with Drake. It didn't take much to know by the way she was walking that he hurt her.

But Cole also knew that if she could do that to him so easily, he guessed he'd have no will power with when it came to her, and anything she wanted.

If she decided to really seduce him, would he be able to resist her? Cole pondered that thought and took into account what had just happened here. He came to his senses about the kissing, but when she went down on him, he had no will power. That told him that the answer to his question was a definite no! So what the hell was he going to do about it? He didn't know. All he did know was that he couldn't claim her. He wasn't going to do that to the family, no matter how many of them told him that it wouldn't be disrespectful. If she seduced him, then she should also be prepared that he would never mark her. Something he was going to make sure she understood tonight, first chance he got.

Chapter Four

Cole and Chase didn't show up for dinner. When the three of them sat down, Drake told them that Cole decided he and Chase were going to town to have a look at things. But Celine knew what was really going on. Cole was avoiding her. Plain and simple. He was so embarrassed over what had happened in the run down cabin that he couldn't face her. Which was fine with her, she just didn't like the whole idea of them going to town. Her gut screamed that he was running and there was a damn good chance he was going to hook up with some girl tonight.

That pissed her off but good!

She wanted Cole to be so on edge that he couldn't fight it when she went to him to finish what she had just got started.

After dinner, Celine helped Carrick with the dishes. She was drying a pan when she thought about pumping her for some information.

"Carrick what was it like the first time you had sex?" Celine asked.

Carrick stopped loading the rest of the dishes into the washer. She was bent over, looking up at her. "Huh?"

"You heard me." Okay, so this was going to be uncomfortable. "What was it like?"

Slowly Carrick stood up. Her mouth was open in shock. "Well, um, let me think. Um, it was in the back of a car, so that wasn't fun."

"And Drake wasn't your first?"

"No," Carrick chuckled. "I um, I went out with this guy my father hired to piss him off. He didn't want me to date, and I knew this guy wanted a—" she met Celine in the eye and cleared her throat. "He, um wanted to go out so I snuck out, we parked, got it on, and got caught."

"By your dad?"

"No, the cops," she nodded, going back to loading the dishwasher up. "Shined the light right on the finishing moment. We zipped up, and were escorted to the front door where the prick rang the bell and I had to meet my father face to face. Man, the look on his face was so worth the beating."

"But what was it like?"

Once more Carrick stopped for a second. She looked like she was trying to recall it. "You know, I don't really remember." She closed the door and turned the washer on. "Back then I was so bent on pissing my father off I think I would have sold my soul if it would bring him down a peg. But that doesn't mean it shouldn't be special," she went on quickly.

"Heather told me that Brock really made her first time something that she will never forget. And that's important. I think of Drake and our first time together as the first."

"Did you start things?"

Carrick dried her hand on a towel before leaning her hip up against the counter. She smiled. "Yeah, I guess I did. I mean I kissed him and that just, I don't know, made things happen."

Celine made a silent O. She thought about what she did to Cole and how he seemed to be avoiding her. Maybe she did cross the line when she went down on him. She didn't know. She was going on instinct, like her mother told her. But now Celine was worried she might have gone too far.

"Why don't you ask me what you really want to ask me," Carrick said.

Celine swallowed hard and met Carrick in the eyes. "Okay." She took a deep breath, licked her lips, and let it out. "How can I seduce Cole into mating and marking me?"

"Celine," Carrick sighed, pushed away from the counter and sitting down at the table. Celine went over with her, taking the seat across from her.

"You can't really force him into doing this. You do know that right?"

"Carrick, what am I supposed to do?" Celine slapped her hands down on the table. "I only have this summer to force his hand and make him do something. This is my only chance."

"Chance at what? Do you want to have him for life or a night? Because I don't see Cole being the kind of guy to just bend to what ever it is you want, Celine. If what all I've been hearing is true, and there is a spark and he has been fighting it this long, what makes you think one night of seducing him is going to change anything?"

"What else do I have?"

Carrick leaned forward, "Ever thought about talking to him?"

* * * *

Celine sat on the steps of the front porch, waiting for Cole and Chase to come home. It was after midnight and the waiting was driving her nuts. All sorts of different things were going through her head. She wondered what he was doing and if he was doing something with some hot girl. Someone who had way more experience than she did.

She was just about to give up and go to bed when headlights off in the distance busted through the night. Celine stiffened and waited.

Cole's jeep pulled into the drive, parked behind Drake's truck and Chase got out of the passengers side. Cole stayed behind the wheel.

"Hey girl, you're up late," Chase said.

Celine tore her eyes from Cole to smile at Chase. "Wanted to talk to Cole."

"Ah," Chase glanced behind him. "Good luck."

Chase kissed her on the cheek before going into the house. Celine stood up and waited for Cole to get out. She didn't even realize she was holding her breath until he opened the door and she let it out in a rush.

Slowly he got out and closed the door. With both hands in his pockets he walked up to her, stopping far enough away from her to hurt.

"Can we talk?" she asked.

"About what?"

"About what happened today."

Cole took a deep breath, his eyes narrowing on her. "Sure, let's talk about that. What the hell were you thinking?" He was pissed. She could hear it in his voice and trying like hell to not let it affect him. "I have one weak moment and kiss you and you instantly go down on your damn knees."

"Jesus, Cole you make it sound so dirty."

"Well it wasn't romantic in my books, Celine."

"So why did you kiss me?" she charged back at him. "I mean, it felt like you wanted something to happen. You were, after all, hard."

"Why the hell shouldn't I have gotten hard? I watched you strip and redress."

Her mouth dropped open. "What?" she gasped.

"Yeah, I saw every inch of your damn backside. What man wouldn't get all hot and bothered looking at an ass like that?" he emphasized with his hand waving in the air towards her.

"Now you're just trying to be crude." She turned and walked up the steps towards the door, but he stopped her.

"No, I'm stating a fact, Celine. You want me, I get that. Do I get excited thinking about spreading you out under me? Sure." He came up behind her, yanking her around by the arm. When she didn't look up at him he also forced her to do that. "Understand me, Celine, and understand what I'm going to tell you real good. I'm not going to mate you." That had her moving her eyes up to his. "So get it out of your head right now. You want to fuck, I'll fuck you in a heart beat. That's it."

He let her go and walked inside, slamming the door on her. Celine stood there, hugging herself. And in silence the tears that formed fell.

* * * *

"That was damn cruel!" Chase growled at Cole when he came inside.

He was waiting for him at the door and turned on Cole. "She didn't deserve that."

"Stay out of it, Chase," Cole growled back.

"No, I'm not going to stay out of it."

Cole brushed past him and took the stairs two at a time. He went right to his room, slamming the door. He was pissed. So pissed at what he had to do that he could just scream. But it had to be done. He couldn't give Celine what she wanted and refused to ruin her life by claiming her.

"What the hell is your problem?" Chase busted into his room, also slamming the door shut.

"Not now, Chase."

"That was bullshit, Cole. I've seen you do a lot of stupid shit, but that was beyond stupid." Chase was huffing, his face red. "How the hell could you crush her like that?"

"Because it's the best thing for her," Cole tossed back, breathing just as hard from his own anger. "I refuse to be anyone's mate when all I have to offer is a hand out!" Cole bit the back of his hand to stop from saying anymore and turned his back on his brother.

"So this all had to do with your damn pride. You would toss everything away and have nothing. Cole I don't understand you anymore."

Cole turned back around, meeting Chase's eyes.

"You use to be someone I looked up." Chase shrugged, "Hell I even used to want to be you. But now I don't even know who you are. You're so angry at the world and anyone that wants to give you an ounce of comfort you think it's a hand out. You want to piss this away? Fine." Chase tossed his hands up in the air before extending them out to him. "Just don't expect me to sit back and do nothing."

"What the hell is that supposed to mean?" Cole frowned.

"You figure it out." Chase turned and left, once more slamming the door closed.

Cole rubbed his face quickly and growled, slapping his legs. He heard the front door bang, went to the window and saw Chase heading for the woods. He kept his eyes on his brother until he couldn't see him anymore, then he turned and sat down on the bed. He hung his head down and resting it in his hands.

Cole didn't know what the hell he was going to do. Did he want Celine? Hell yeah! But he wasn't right for her. He had nothing to offer her, nothing that he'd earned himself. Everything he had was given to him. Hell, he didn't even have a home. What was he going to do, mate her and live with Drake? Yeah, that would be great. They could take turns out screaming each other during sex on the full moon.

Yeah, great way to live.

Standing back up he undressed for bed. Down to his boxer/briefs, Cole stretched out in the middle of the bed, arm over his eyes. He heard the door open slowly and stiffened. Biting his lip, Cole waited for her to make her move, not at all surprised that she was making it. You didn't go head to head with a Draeger without them trying to come back at you.

Cole refused to look at her. It was bad enough that his damn dick was hard, making, he was pretty sure, a nice size tent in his briefs. It was a fight, one damn hard one when he felt the bed shift by his feet. She was crawling on the bed—crawling between his legs—drawing closer.

"Cole, look at me," Celine said.

He knew he was going to be making a big ass mistake, but Cole moved his arm and looked up at her. He swore under his breath, because what he saw was definitely going to crack the shell he was working so damn hard to put around himself.

She was dressed in hardly a thing; low riding lace panties with a flowing lace that had one string holding the damn thing closed. Her long hair was loose down her back, and those blue eyes of hers were wide open, waiting for him to make his move.

Slowly he sat up, but he kept telling himself to not touch her. If he made any kind of contract with her, then he was a goner.

"You need to leave," he managed to get out, fisting his hands in the covers under him.

She moved from between his legs to straddle his lap, chest right up in his face, arms hanging over his shoulders. "I don't want to leave."

"Celine, you don't want to do this," he said between his teeth.

She rubbed against him and Cole closed his eyes at the pleasure. Damn if she wasn't testing his control to the max.

"Yes I do," she breathed close to his lips. Her hands fisted into his hair, pulling his head back.

Cole kept his eyes closed, refusing to look at her. If he opened his eyes, then things were going to get way out of his control. "I want you to be my first, my only lover." She kissed him lightly on the lips. "Don't fight what's between us, Cole. You'll only lose." Again she kissed him.

Cole shook his head. "I can't give you what you want." He couldn't stop himself from wrapping both arms around her, holding her closer. "I can't and won't claim you." He gave up the fight and kissed her deep, thrusting his tongue into her mouth. He moved his hands down to her ass, squeezing the flesh and moaning into her mouth. Damn if she didn't feel good in his arms—so right.

Cole gripped her hips and stood her up. She stood on the bed, legs parted, lips swollen from the deep rough kissing. He grabbed her panties and slid them down her legs where she stepped out of them. They dropped to the floor and he skimmed back up her legs around to her ass, bringing her close to his face.

He closed his eyes and took a deep breath, smelling her sweet scent. One kiss was all he was going to do. One small innocent touch and then he was going to toss her pretty ass out of his room.

But Cole should have known better than that. He wasn't going to get off that easy. Nope. That one touch ended up being a kiss, then a lick. Before he knew what the hell he was doing he had her sweet pussy pressing in his face and his tongue was lapping at every sweet bit of cream that she produced.

Her taste was addicting. He couldn't get enough of it, couldn't get his tongue deep enough inside her, couldn't drink enough. When she tried to pull away from him, he growled and dug his fingers into the flesh of her ass. Cole knew that the hold he had on her more than likely was hurting and bruising her, but he couldn't help himself. He had to have it. When he found her swollen clit and brought that into his mouth, she cried out, pulling at his hair until the pain turned to intense pleasure.

He wanted more. Fuck he wanted to sit there and just eat at her all night long. But the pounding in his cock was intensifying. No longer did he think he couldn't. No, now he knew he had to have her at least once. He needed to have the memories of the way she felt and tasted.

Cole nudged at her legs to lower her back down onto his lap. Quickly he freed his cock from his briefs, positioned it and hissed when the sensitive head touched the wet lips of heaven.

Slowly he lowered her down, feeling the tight muscles of her vagina stretch for his thick size. Man, she was so damn tight that Cole knew without a doubt that this was going to be a very short ride for him. Not only had it felt like forever since he'd had sex, but he was having his first virgin. He never knew how tight one could be, until now.

Her nails dug into his shoulders as he kept lowering her down on him. He wanted to see her face, watch the expression that came across as he filled her tight pussy with his aching cock. But Cole couldn't stop from watching the actual scene itself. Witnessing her taking it and feeling the stretching heightened his pleasure by ten.

He stopped when he felt the one thing he knew without a doubt was a gift—her virginity. Cole groaned softly and growled. His cock throbbed, matching the pounding in his chest. He was very excited about breaking through it. Of taking it and branding her his. But he couldn't. Cole couldn't mark her his forever, and as much as he hated to admit it, it broke his heart a bit. That alone gave him pause to go no further with this.

"I can't do this Celine," he whispered. "This belongs to your mate."

Again she fisted her hands into his hair, yanking his head back so he was looking up at her. "You are my mate."

Celine kissed him deep and pushed herself down the rest of the way onto him. She cried out. A muffled sound, thanks to the deep kiss she was giving him.

Cole closed his eyes and kissed her back. He couldn't fight this. He couldn't stop her from moving up and down on him, or stop his tongue from matching the rhythm. He held onto her hips, grinding her on his cock when she came down. There was no stopping him from fucking her like he wanted.

With one hand, he reached up and yanked the ribbon that was holding her shirt closed. He closed that hand over one breast, broke the kiss, and took a hard nipple into his mouth. He sucked the hard nub, pulled on it and moaned when he felt her pussy clamp down on his cock at the same time. He was close. So close it was killing him. Celine whimpered, and her arms went around his neck tight. She kissed at his neck, licked and nipped at him, not missing one beat of motion. She took him just about as fast and hard as he would have taken her if she was under him.

"Oh, oh, oh," she panted right before she tightened around him.

That was all it took. Cole tossed his head back, slamming her down and holding her in place. He didn't yell like he wanted, but bit the inside of his mouth to hold the sound back. His cock convulsed, making her pussy feel extra tight around him. The urge to bite her shoulder was ever so strong, but he fought it. He wasn't going to do that. Couldn't. Celine deserved someone better than him.

He dropped back down on the bed and she slid from on top of him to sit up on the side of the bed, her back to him. Cole was breathing hard, as was she. He glanced at her back, reached out to touch her, but stopped. He didn't know what to say or do. He couldn't give her what she wanted.

Celine bent over and picked something up. Still saying nothing, he watched her slip her panties back on then rose to her feet. With her head lowered, she tied the ribbon of her top, closing it.

She walked to the door and it seemed that when she touched the knob he found his voice. "Celine—"

But she didn't say anything or look at him. The door opened silently and closed just as quietly.

"Shit," he sighed, fixing his own clothes before getting under the covers. "Shit, shit, shit!" he growled when he heard the water start in the bathroom. Celine was in there, he just knew it.

* * * *

Chase sat at the foot of his bed, one knee bent with a photo in his hand of a blonde girl. Sasha! He couldn't sleep. He was pissed at Cole for the way he was treating Celine, and trying to decide what to do with his own future. But why the hell was he looking at a photo of a kid was beyond him. He looked up when he heard the shower start up. A quick glance at the clock, which read two in the morning, and Chase was putting the photo down and standing up. He glanced out the window before cracking the bedroom door. One single light was coming from under the bathroom door.

Chase waited and it wasn't long before Celine came out of the bathroom in her robe. He could tell right off that she was crying about something. When she went into her own room, Chase opened the door further and left his room to go to hers. He knocked softly but when she didn't answer he opened the door and stepped inside, closing it.

"Celine? You okay?"

The room was dark, but he could still see her form on the bed, curled up in a ball. He also heard her crying. Chase didn't think. He went to her, sitting down on the side of the bed. He touched her shoulder and made her roll over. Once she was facing him, she sat up and wrapped her arms around his neck, hugging and crying on him.

Chase held her, rocking her like one would a child. Even though she took a shower, he could pick up the faint scent of Cole. She must have gone to him and what ever happened went very wrong.

"What'd he do?" Chase asked softly.

Celine didn't answer him, only shook her head and fisted her hands in his shirt. He felt it get soaked from her crying and held her tighter. *Damn you, Cole!*

"He's a stubborn ass, Celine."

She pulled back some, her face wet. "He doesn't want me," she sniffed. "Not even after I gave him—"

Chase pressed his fingers over her mouth. He didn't want to hear what she gave him. He didn't need to know. "He wants you, Celine. He's just too damn stupid to see it. But that's okay." He wiped the tears from her cheeks, giving her a big smile. "We're going to make him see it. The hard way."

"I don't understand." She frowned.

"I know you don't." He reached over for the towel and cleaned her face up. "But you will. I think its time you and I give dear Cole a taste of reality." She kept frowning at him and Chase rolled his eyes at her. "We are going to act like we're dating."

Her mouth dropped open. "How's that going to help?"

"Oh, trust me." He picked up both of her hands, kissing them. "It's going to drive him so nuts, that Cole will have no choice but to put his claim on you." He winked.

"Guaranteed."

* * * *

"And you think this hair-brained idea of yours is really going to work?" Drake asked.

Chase woke Celine up early and had her meet him downstairs before Drake took off for town. One look at Celine and Drake knew without a doubt something was wrong.

"You know, I was wondering the same thing," Celine added.

Drake was leaning on the counter, a mug of coffee in his hand. Since it was six in the morning Carrick was still in bed, and it seemed like Cole was as well. Perfect for Chase. He wanted to get the ball rolling quickly. He wanted his brother to claim his mate before the up coming full moon.

"I don't have a single doubt about it," Chase said. "Once he thinks I'm dating her, he'll go nuts."

"He might also beat the shit out of you," Drake snickered. He took a drink, finishing it all, then placing the cup in the sink. "Okay then. If you really think this is going to work."

"I also want you to take us to town," Chase added. "I've been giving some thought about the space around here and once Cole thinks I'm dating Celine its going to start to get very tense."

"What-cha got in mind?" Drake asked.

"Couple things." Chase answered. "Want my own transportation, and I want to put a trailer on the ground Natasha gave me." He shrugged, "Time I had my own space."

Drake's eyebrows went up, "Really? I was under the impression you two didn't want to take anything from my grandmother."

"Natasha treated us like we were one of her kids. I'll admit I'm not too crazy about it, but figured everyone needs a little help to get set up. I have my own dreams and goals, Drake. Not going to get them if I don't take the help that is right in front of me."

"Smartest thing either one of you have ever said." Drake nodded. "Okay, let's go to town. Dying to see what you're going to pick out." He smiled.

"So am I." Celine added. "And to see how this plan of yours goes."

Chase stood up from the table and smiled. "Don't worry so much. And put some jeans or shorts on. Something tight and hot. After all, we are trying to drive my dear sweet brother nuts you know."

Celine smiled, "This is so going to back fire on you."

"Let me just say if it works, then you owe me one."

"Five minutes, CeeCee," Drake held up his hand and she took off. Once she was gone, Drake turned his full attention on Chase. "Do you really think this plan is going to work? And don't bullshit me either. I know you're trying to make her feel better."

"It'll work Drake," Chase sighed. "When he heard from my own mouth that I thought Celine turned out to be one hell of a woman he growled. A man doesn't growl like that if he isn't interested or wants a girl. He just doesn't think he has anything to offer her since what he owns right now was handed to him."

"Ahhh," Drake nodded, crossing his arms over his chest, "Now I think I understand. This isn't just about pride, but about self worth. Came from nothing—"

"Has nothing," Chase finished.

"What he needs is my foot up his ass," Drake grumbled.

"No, this will work better."

"Chase I don't know if you are a genius or an idiot." Drake shrugged and pushed away from the counter. "Time will tell."

"Okay I'm ready." Celine came back into the kitchen and Chase just stared at her.

He didn't lie when he said she was one hell of a woman. In fact, she was drop dead gorgeous. She went back up and changed into a pair of pink shorts that were very short and a tight tank top with thin straps. Sneakers on her feet, hair pulled back in a tail at the base of her neck. Yep, a knock out!

"Something wrong?" She asked, snapping him out of staring.

"Not yet," Chase answered.

Drake laughed and slapped him on the back. "Remind me again who I'm going to have to worry about?"

"Funny," Chase mumbled.

They headed to town where the first stop was a bike shop. Chase fell in love right off with a Kawasaki Ninja ZX-10R all black. He took it for a test run and then bought it. His next stop was to purchase a new leather jacket and helmet with a dark visor. Drake was going to leave him until

Chase told him that he wanted his help with the trailer.

They were directed to a place out of town that sold all kinds and all size of campers, RVs and trailers. They looked at several and Chase was about to think it was a bad idea and that he wasn't going to find one he liked until Celine yelled she had the perfect one. Weekend Warrior is what it was called and what had Chase agreeing with her was the small storage or garage at the end of it. It was twelve feet long, plenty of room for his bike and even had a built in washer and dryer in the room. Past the sliding doors was an overhead loft bed. To his left, the front door and right in front was the combo of kitchen/living room.

The kitchen space had the usual, a corner sink, flat top stove with oven, built in fridge with top freezer, cabinets and this one had a small island. It even had a floor to ceiling pantry. Across the space was a built in leather sofa that folded out to a queen size bed if needed. Next to that was a table with wrap around seating. Both had over the head storage cabinets.

Down a small hall, up three steps and to the right was the bathroom. It wasn't small, either. It had a nice size shower, toilet and sink with counter top and storage above and below. Further down the hall was the bedroom with another queen size bed, closet, built in television over a dresser and a counter top space around the top part of the bed. All the wood was done in oak, and all the sofas and one chair in the corner next to the front door was done in black leather with zebra stripes in the middle. Bathroom and kitchen had a white marble feel to it.

"Well I swear I've never seen a camper like this before," Drake said, looking around, opening cabinet doors.

"I like it," Chase stated with a shrug.

"I do too," Celine agreed, smiling. "I ever get pissed at Cole I can bunk up there," she thumbed to the loft.

"You know that might not be such a bad idea," Chase chuckled. "Do you know how crazy he would go if you didn't come home?"

"Okay you two, jumping the gun here," Drake held up his hands. "You do realize that if you get this, we are going to have to work our asses off to get the lighting and plumbing on the ground up and working for it? Could take a week or more."

"Drake, money talks and bullshit walks." Chase patted him on the shoulders. "Let me work on that, I just need you to hall this baby over there. Can you do that for me?"

Drake rubbed his chin like he was thinking. "Doesn't look like I've got much of a choice. But you're the one that's gong to have to break this news to your brother especially since he doesn't want you two to take anything from my grandmother."

"Oh, you let me handle him." Chase crossed his arms over his chest.

Chapter Five

"Take it all back!" Cole snapped at Chase, who was packing up his things.

Cole woke up with the intent to talk to Celine about what happened last night. He felt bad. Really bad. But that guilt slipped away real fast when he discovered that she went with Drake and Chase to town.

Carrick told him when he went into the kitchen that Drake had called her to let her know that Chase was going to be moving out. That the three of them left very early in the morning.

He didn't have a good feeling about it either. Celine was running away, something that she never did. Which meant his gut was right about him doing a cluster fuck. They needed to talk. But what was he going to say to her? How was he going to say he was sorry for taking what she should have given to her mate?

You are her mate you stubborn prick! But that wasn't what pissed him off. Now, seeing Chase pull up in the drive on a bike with Celine hanging onto him had Cole seeing red! He couldn't decide though what pissed him off the most. Chase being on that fucking bike or her holding him? Her!

Soon Chase was packing. "I'm not taking it back," Chase said, shoving the last pile of clothes in his bag.

Cole brushed past Chase to pick up the other bags he had waiting by the door. "We agreed to this Chase!" Cole yelled. "We were only going to take the necessities here, not get greedy."

"When did we agree?" Chase yelled back, stopping in the hallway, glaring at him. "I never agreed to shit Cole. You don't want to take the help, fine. That's your choice," he shrugged. "But I'm going to take it. I'm going to do what I want for a change."

"What the hell is that supposed to mean?"

Chase took a deep breath, slinging one of the bags over his shoulder, "Cole, you have everything and you're too damn pigheaded to see it. All our lives I've been doing what is right and what you expected me to do. I stayed in school when I wanted to go to work. I finished school. Then I came out here with you. And I don't have any problem with it," he quickly added when Cole opened his mouth to point out he had never objected to it. "But I want my own life, my own space and, one day, my own mate. You act like you don't want any of that."

"I want it Chase. I just don't want it handed to me," Cole said through his teeth.

"And that's where we differ." Chase turned and went towards the stairs, going down. "I'm not opposed to having help. And I would love to have my mate given to me. Make things a hell of a lot easier!"

Cole growled and followed Chase down and out the front door. What he didn't see with the bike was a small closed trailer hitched to it. Celine was standing next to the bike, looking damn mouth-watering delicious. Damn, he just wanted to take her back to his room and kiss every inch of her body. Since she didn't look at him, Cole stayed put on the porch. She helped Chase put his bags in the trailer, then when he got on the bike she got on behind him.

It just fueled his blood to see her wrap her arms around his brother and not look at him. The bike was turned and right before Chase took off she glanced over her shoulder at him. Cole's gut dropped. He saw her pain, the hurt, and disappointment in her eyes. And he didn't know what the hell to do about it.

"You know I always thought you guys were supposed to be smart or something."

Cole didn't look at Carrick behind him. His eyes were on Celine's back as she rode off with his brother.

"Don't start with me, Carrick."

"I'm not starting anything," she sighed. "Just stating how I see things. You don't step up and piss it all away, that girl is going to go quickly to another. She's too damn pretty to say alone for long."

Cole turned around, "What the fuck do you want me to do?"

There were many things that he had learned to expect with the family since they were taken in, but the hand that came across his face so hard, knocking him back a step, was one he would have never seen coming.

"Wake the fuck up, you dip shit," she snapped, grabbing hold of the front of his shirt, shaking him. "You piss her away I'm really going to kick your ass. In case you think I might not be able to handle your shit because you're this wolf thing, like Drake, he's ten times stronger than you and I can take his ass out." She shoved him away, eyes narrowed on him. "Fix this before it's too damn late. The full moon is right around the corner."

"And what the hell am I supposed to do?" he asked through his teeth, seething with anger over being slapped. But he had enough respect for her not to fight back. Carrick was a girl after all. A human one at that.

"You're smart, Cole." She turned her back on him, opening the front door and going in. "Open your damn eyes and watch how the game is being played."

Cole rubbed his face, thinking about what Carrick said. Okay, so she had a small point, but why the slap? You needed it maybe? "Shut-up," he grumbled to himself, digging into his pocket for the jeep keys.

He got into the driver seat and took off for Chase's property. Instead of coming out of the clearing so they knew he was there, Cole parked in the trees and got out. He walked to the edge, leaned against a tree with his arm overhead and just watched.

Chase had also bought a camper. Drake was helping him set it up and Celine was unpacking the small trailer hitched to the bike. She was laughing and smiling at the two, who were on top of the camper hooking up wires.

Damn she was gorgeous! It was hard for him to believe that mere hours ago he had her in his arms, touching and loving her like he always dreamed. Instead of doing the right thing he'd fucked it all up. He should have marked her last night and made her his forever. But no. He let his damn pride get in the way of things. Like it always seemed to do lately.

She disappeared inside the camper through a ramp that was lowered. This was a camper that Cole had never seen before. It almost looked like it was a garage of some kind.

"What am I going to do?" he groaned to himself.

Chase got down from the top, went inside where Celine was. Cole held his breath, wondering like hell what was going on inside. After a few seconds, Chase's head came out from the front door and Drake also came down. They all went inside, shutting Cole off from discovering anything that might be useful to him. He needed to know how to fix this mess that he was in, but had no clue. How the hell could he fix what was so wrong between him and Celine, and do it before the full moon?

* * * *

"Do you really think he was out there watching us?" Celine asked, peeking out the small window towards the woods.

"Yep," Drake and Chase answered together.

"I've got a bad feeling about this, Chase," she said, straightening up and going over to the small bar where food was in a box. Chase was putting it up in the cabinets and Drake was lounging back on the sofa, legs stretched out, ankles crossed. "If he blows up—"

"Then he'll put a claim on you," Drake stated. He was flipping through a magazine appearing like he didn't have a care in the world. "Because if he doesn't then I'm going to have to hurt him for what he did to you."

She rolled her eyes at him. "It was my fault Drake, not his. I shouldn't have gone into his room and forced him. I should've known better, after all I do know what happens when you try to force one of you guys into doing something you don't want to do."

"Not buying that one," Drake stated, turning a page.

"Oh come on, Drake," Chase said, getting Drake's full attention. "We all know how your Uncle Dedrick refused to do the right thing with her mother."

Drake pointed a finger at Chase, "Not the point I'm trying to make here."

"Then what is the point?" Celine sat down in the chair placed one leg over the other and crossed her arms over her chest.

"My point is that if Cole is going to fight this whole mate thing, then he shouldn't have touched you. Plain and simple." He licked his thumb and turned a page.

Celine lost it and laughed, "If that isn't the most hypocritical thing I've ever heard. You almost lost Carrick because of your sense of need for revenge."

"That's different," he stated.

"No it isn't!" Celine and Chase said at the same time.

Drake closed the magazine and stood up. "I think it's time I head home."

Celine laughed, "Oh, did I say something you didn't like?"

Drake dropped the magazine and left the camper. Celine giggled and Chase went back to unpacking the food.

"So what's the next step to your great plan?" Celine asked.

Chase finished with the last box then brought out two sodas from the fridge. He handed one to her before sitting down on the sofa, legs stretched out. "I'm thinking a late night dinner. You dress up hot, make sure he sees it and heads over here."

"You really are serious about this whole dating thing?"

"Yep. Time someone showed my hard headed brother the light."

Celine shook her head and stood up, "Okay. I just hope you're right about this because I don't see him changing his mind at all."

Chase winked at her. "Trust me. And wear that pink dress. It drove him nuts."

Celine went back to the house. She snuck in and up to her room. Cole's jeep wasn't in the drive and it worried her. She wasn't sure what to think about him being gone, but was glad he was. She didn't want to face him. Couldn't. Not after what happened last night.

She really thought that going to him and giving herself to him would change things. That he would claim her like it was meant to be. But he didn't.

Sure, he had sex with her. What man in their right might would turn down the chance to be some girl's first? But it just hurt that after she showed him they were perfect for each other that he would still hold back. Celine knew without a doubt that Cole wanted to claim her. She could feel it. And now that Chase explained to her why Cole was being so reluctant she understood. But understanding didn't lessen the hurt.

She changed into the pink dress. Off in the distance she heard thunder and saw some lightning. A storm to match the moods of everyone it seemed.

When she was ready to leave she heard Cole's jeep pull up. Biting her lip, Celine went to the window to watch him. Damn he was hot! Why the hell couldn't he just get over it and do what they both knew the other wanted.

Deciding that she would never get the answer she wanted, she turned from the window and left her room. By the time she reached the bottom of the stairs, Cole walked inside.

"Where're you going?" he demanded.

"Out." Celine moved around him, only to be stopped by him taking hold of her arm.

"There's a storm heading our way, and you shouldn't be out in it." She tried to jerk her arm from his hand, but he held it tighter. "And definitely not dressed in that dress."

"Cole you're not my mate, or did you forget that you fucked me, but didn't mark me?" This time when she yanked at her arm, he let her go. "Now if you don't mind, which I don't give a shit if you do. I have a date and I'm going to be late."

"A date!" he yelled, following her outside. "Who the hell are you dating?"

"None of your damn business."

She heard Cole suck in his breath. Then Cole's hard hands grabbed from behind and forced her to face him. "Oh, I think it is my business. I have a right to know who you are going to be dating since it was me who broke you in."

Celine slugged him right in the jaw, almost knocking him down. "You go to hell Cole Sexton. You made it very clear you didn't want me."

She didn't give him time to say anymore. Celine took off running towards Chase's place, fearing that Cole might be right behind her. He wasn't.

She rushed all the way to the camper and went inside. Chase was cooking and stopped, turning with a frown to her.

"What's wrong?" he asked.

"Cole saw me leaving and didn't like the whole date idea," she huffed out, moving to the sofa to sit down, holding her side. "In fact I would say he was pretty pissed at the idea."

"Good." He went back to cooking. "He needs to get pissed."

"Chase I'm not so sure about this idea. I've got a funny feeling."

"I wouldn't let it bother you too much," Chase filled two plates with a pasta dish he'd made and took them over to the table. "Why don't you go to the bathroom and wash up. Dinner is ready and after we eat then we can talk about the next mode of action."

She smiled, stood up and went to the small hallway, up three steps and into the bathroom on the right. She turned the water on and was about to wash her face when she heard pounding on the door.

Celine didn't need an announcement to know who it was. Cole! She heard muffled talking and then his voice raising. Jumping with the thunder, Celine decided to go with the plan that Chase came up with and let Cole see who she was dating. She stepped out of the bathroom, held her breath, and waited for him to explode.

Cole's eyes landed on her and Celine would have sworn on a bible that his face turned red. Slowly she closed the bathroom door and walked down the three steps back into the living-kitchen area. Chase hung his head and backed up, giving Cole space.

"This is your date?" Cole yelled. "My mother-fucking brother!"

"Yes," she answered with as much calm as she could.

"Son-of-a-bitch!"

"Cole—" Chase started to say.

Cole held up his finger at Chase but his eyes were on Celine. "Don't say a word. Not one word."

"Well, what the hell did you expect?" Celine threw at him. "You toss me away and I'm not supposed to be with anyone?"

"No, you're not supposed to go out with my brother!"

"Says who?"

"Me!" Cole yelled at the top of his lungs.

Celine walked right up to him, mere inches from touching his chest with her own. "Well that's just too damn bad since you don't have a pot to piss in where I'm concerned." She moved around him to the door. More thunder boomed and another flash of lightning hit. "Sorry about dinner, Chase, but I've lost my appetite." She left before more could be said, but it wasn't too long before she wasn't alone.

"Celine!" Cole yelled. "Damn-it, don't you walk away from me."

"Go to hell Cole!" she yelled over her shoulder.

The thunder and lightning came faster with the promise of a hard rain any moment. Celine picked up her pace, almost running to get back to the house.

She heard his footsteps behind her getting quicker. So she took off running from him. She didn't want to talk, didn't want to hear his excuses as to why she would never be his.

"Celine!"

The rain came down, muffling her name a bit, soaking her to the skin. She slipped twice and on the third went down. Before she could get up, Cole was upon her, flipping her over and pinning her down. The rain beat on her face to mix with fresh hurtful tears.

"Why. Just tell me why?" Cole demanded.

"You don't want me." The statement seemed to give him pause. Celine hit him in the chest and cried with the rain beating on her. "You don't want me."

His hands went to her face, holding her, giving her a light shake. "Fuck, I want you more than you know," he growled. "I want you so damn bad I hurt and have been for ten damn years. Don't you know that?"

Celine shook her head and tried to twist out from under him, but he didn't let her go.

Cole lowered his body to hers, pinning her to the ground. "But I have nothing that is mine to offer you," he breathed out, resting his forehead against hers.

"None of that has ever mattered to me," she sniffed. "Don't you get that? I don't give a shit if we live in a tent, as long as you're holding me at night."

Cole kissed her, his hands still holding her face. Celine wrapped her arms around his waist, kissing him back, fighting a tongue duel. The rain beat on them, but did little to cool her heated flesh. Celine felt like she was starving for him, and couldn't get close enough or hold him tight enough.

Cole kissed her deep, slid one hand down the side of her body, up her dress where he ripped her panties from her body. Celine moaned into his mouth and arched her body closer. She parted her legs for him. He rubbed her aching pussy and she went to work at freeing the hard cock that she hungered for.

She was wet. Could feel it and prayed as they kissed that he wouldn't be gentle or easy. She was on fire, in agonizing need and just wanted to be taken the way a male shifter would take his mate when claiming her.

Cole growled and slammed full force into her, just like she wanted.

Shifters 5: Cole's Awakening

Celine broke the kiss and screamed, coming at the same time. She hugged him as tightly as she could, digging her nails into his wet shirt that covered back. Her whole body shook and she couldn't seem to get air into her lungs from the orgasm.

Nothing she'd ever done had felt this powerful, this good and it sure as hell had her wanting more of everything right now. She fisted one hand in his hair while he kissed at her neck, moving in and out of body like a man driven insane. He was relentless in how he entered and left her body, and Celine loved every second of it.

"Don't stop," she pleaded, shaking her head back and forth and squirming under him.

"Please don't ever stop."

He kissed her shoulder, teasing her by sucking, licking, and nipping at the tender flesh where his mark would be. Celine couldn't stop herself from using her muscles to try to hold him in place and couldn't stop her whimper from slipping past her lips at the sensitivity she was feeling.

Each time he thrust back inside her, what little amount of air she had in her lungs rushed out. Pure, raw pleasure gripped her and didn't let go. Cole stroked her inner flesh with so much skill it amazed her. The manner in which he loved her body told her enough. He loved her just as much as she loved him.

Celine welcomed the burning between her legs from his roughness. He was so thick that she could actually feel the unused muscles of her vagina stretching to the max for him, it was just another thing that she wouldn't change no matter what.

"Yes," she moaned with each thrust, each grind on her clit. She felt the wakening of another orgasm, this one promising to be unlike anything she ever thought to experience. "Oh God it's coming!"

Faster. Harder. Cole pushed her closer and closer until she knew for a fact she was going to die from the pleasure. Celine always wondered if it was possible to die from pleasure, and knew it had to be true. No one could withstand this and not think that they had departed to another place.

"Cole, Cole, Cole!" she panted his name, reaching for it.

And it came

Celine screamed. Her orgasm rippled through her system, blinding her with pleasure. Off in the distance she heard Cole cry out, felt his cock swell inside her and felt his mouth on her shoulder. The bite burned and hurt, but she didn't mind. Celine gasped and smiled at the same time. She held him close, eyes closed with the rain still beating down on them.

"I love you, Cole," she sighed, relaxing under him.

He released her shoulder to nuzzle her neck, kissing his way up to her ear. "I love you too, Celine. Have since you were twelve." He slipped his hands under her, holding her as tightly as she clung to him. "And if you or my brother ever try to pull shit like that again I'm going to beat your ass."

Celine giggled. "I might enjoy that."

* * * *

Chase smiled as he paced his small living room, talking to Drake on his cell. "Yep. Worked like a dream. He went out of here like hell was on his ass for her."

"Are you sure he's going to mark her and finish this damn claim?" Drake asked on the other end.

"With the look on his face when he saw her over here? Without a doubt."

"Well if he doesn't, then I'm gong to put my foot in your ass before I kick his." Drake hung up and Chase smiled.

He shook his head, quickly finished the dishes and putting the left over food in the fridge. Chase then went back for a quick shower and to relax in his bed. But he was anything but relaxed as he lay in the middle, listening to the rain beat down on the camper. His mind was on Jada, and on what she might be doing.

She hadn't called in a few days. That had him worrying. He knew her too well and was pretty damn sure she wasn't stopping like she promised him. That meant he was going to have to go out looking for her. Damn! Cole sure as hell wasn't going to like that idea.

"Shit Jada, you're going to be the death of me." Chase got back up out of bed and started to pack himself a small bag. Come morning, he was going to go out and find her sorry ass before she got it shot off, or worst. Killed.

* * * *

They were in his bed, facing the window, watching the rain pour down. The moon was almost full, though you couldn't see it due to the overcast sky, Cole was rubbing Celine's back, resting on his side with his head in his hand. Once he was able to stand up, they made it back to the house and went right up to the bathroom. Together they took a shower. They didn't have sex again, but lay down in Cole's snug, warm bed. He wanted her again, but held it back. Full moon was right around the corner, which meant she was going to need her rest and energy.

"So what's it like?" Celine asked, with drowsiness in her voice.

"What?"

"Your heat?" She sighed, turning her head to look at him. "What does it feel like?"

"I feel on edge." He touched her face, moving her hair behind her ear before laying down and putting his arm around her.

"That's it?"

He shook his head, "No, I have this need that I can't seem to get rid of. Like an itch that has no way of being scratched away. I want, and there isn't anything that can take the want away."

"Does it hurt?"

"It has." He picked up a long strand of her hair. It was still damp from her shower. "But it all feels very different now."

"How so?"

He sighed before dropping his arm over her again. "I feel the edge, but I also pick up this sense of peace. The animal in me knows that I have my mate so he can come out and relieve the tension that he has held in for so long."

She smiled, "Are you going to change on me?"

Cole also smiled. "You want me to?"

She turned in his arms, facing him and got closer, snuggling up to him. Her tongue came out of her mouth and licked under his chin right up to his lips. "Yeah I do," she whispered. "I want to feel the animal come out while you take me." He growled and she rubbed against him. "I don't want you to hold anything back either. You do…" Her hand went under the covers and wrapped around his cock, taking his breath from him, "Then I won't suck this and I love tasting you." She nipped at his lip and his cock grew thicker in her hand. "I want to suck on you like a lollipop, just like I did in the cabin. I want to hear you yell as you come."

Cole chuckled, only because he couldn't think about doing anything else. "Don't tease me Celine."

"Did your last girlfriend go down on you?"

"I haven't had a girlfriend in over five years," he groaned when she started to stroke him. "Ever since you kissed me at your party I couldn't date anyone else without thinking about you."

"Hum." She nuzzled his neck, stroked him a few more times before stopping and turning her back to him. "I think I'm going to get some sleep instead."

"Oh, really!" Cole started tickling her until she turned back around to face him. He pinned her to him, holding her tight with one arm, and brushing her hair off her face with the other hand. "You're a dream come true, Celine," he spoke softly. "I never thought I would have you in my bed or arms like I have you now. You were a dream so far out of my reach."

Her chin went up and a twinkle was in her eyes, "I guess you better keep a hold of me then, huh?'

He kissed the tip of her nose, "I never plan on letting you go. You're stuck with me mate, until I die."

"I'm going to hold you to that promise," she sighed, her eyes drooping slightly. "And I love it when you say mate. Do it again."

He smiled, "Mate."

"Again."

He kissed her, brushing his lips across her own, "Mate," he whispered. "My sweet, sweet, very sexy mate, who I love very much."

She smiled. A bright big smile that he knew he would never get tired of seeing. "And in the morning you make up with Chase?" she asked.

Cole groaned and dropped down on his back, arms over his head. She came over him, or more like lay right on top of his body. "What do I get out of it?"

She bit his nipple and he jumped. "Ouch! You little shit."

"You don't make things right with Chase, who was only doing this so you would wake up, and your heat is going to be the least of your worries."

Cole slid his hands down her back to cup her rear. Damn he loved her body. Loved everything about her. Made him wonder why the hell he was so damn stubborn about the claim.

"You think your dad is going to be okay with this?" he asked, kneading her flesh. He thought about the moment he was going to take her there. It was one of those dark wet dreams of his.

"As long as you do the right thing, you're safe." She grinned.

"And what might the right thing be, Ms. Celine?" He cocked his head to the side. "Marking you, or calling the council and letting them know your plan worked?" A few seconds went by, along with another crack of thunder before her mouth opened and her eyes got wide.

"You knew!" She sat up on him, straddling his hips. "How could you know about the request?"

He smiled at her, and put his hands under his head, enjoying the view of her bare breasts. "They sent me a letter."

"I can't believe you knew this whole time and didn't say a word to me about it."

Cole ran the back of his hand down her breast to her leg. "You know sitting like that right now with the anger in your eyes is hot. Right now all I can think about is watching your breasts jiggle as you fuck me."

Celine narrowed her eyes on him and crossed her arms over her breasts, hiding them. She started to move off him, but Cole stopped her.

She shook her head. "Nope. As punishment for not telling me you knew about the claim, you have to wait. No more for you until your heat."

"Ah, come on!"

She got off of him and pulled the sheet up to her chest.

"You can't be serious?" Celine gave her back to him and he chuckled. "Celine, you can't do this to me. Not now."

"Good night, Cole."

"Celine…" He snuggled up close to her, pressing his lips right up to her ear. "You have me hot, hard, and very horny. I'm prepared to play dirty if I have to." He moved his hand down her back and between her legs from behind. She was wet.

"Cole!" she gasped, grabbing his wrist, trying to pull him away.

He pushed two fingers deep into her and sucked on her earlobe. "I'm going to fuck you, and I'm going to do it right now."

Before she could protest, Cole yanked the sheet away, grabbed her hips, pulled her up so she was on her hands and knees, and thrust into her. Celine moaned loudly and he hissed. Damn she was tight. So fucking tight, it felt like a fist wrapped around his dick.

He took her hard, slapping into her fast, rocking the bed with his strokes. She gasped with each penetration, had her hands fisted into the bedding. Five years of having nothing, and going back to great sex had Cole feeling like he was a young boy out to get laid all the time.

It was a quick ride. Very quick. Her pussy clamped down on him, she cried out, but muffled it in the blankets and Cole came with her. He collapsed on top of her, panting but feeling so damn good. *Why the hell did he fight it so much? Because you're a dumb-ass?*

"You sure you want a man with an appetite like this who has nothing?" he asked, breathing hard. "I might fuck you into an early grave."

Celine laughed softly. "Try it. The next ride is me on you."

He kissed her back then licked up to her neck where he closed his mouth over her shoulder on his mark. He bit it but not as hard as what he normally would do if he was in the heat of the moment.

"I'm looking forward to it," he said in her ear before wrapping his arms tightly around her body. "Now get some sleep before I change my mind and have my way with you."

She yawned. "Promises, promises."

Chapter Six

"I say we force him, *my* way!" Jason stood in Josh's office. He was just as pissed off as the rest of them. "Kane needs to know *we* are in charge, not him!"

Josh watched Jason pacing his office. The man was on edge a lot more than normal. Josh also noticed he was looking for all kinds of excuses lately to beat Kane. His appetite for pain and suffering was becoming a concern.

"What are you suggesting?" Josh asked.

"We have that girl still drugged. I was told she's ovulating so let's try it again. If he holds back on us we make it known that it's either him or Sasha."

Josh sat back in his chair and linked his fingers together over his chest. "You just beat him. How do you expect him to perform now?"

Jason leaned over the desk. "We have the drugs."

After a lengthy amount of time thinking, Josh nodded. "Okay. We'll try it again."

Jason smiled. They walked down to the lab together. Even after the beating Jason gave him, Kane still paced his cage. The chains around his neck were clanking loudly and drops of blood were all over the floor from his back. Kane stopped when he saw the two of them approach. Jason took the dart gun that a guard handed to him. He aimed and shot Kane in the leg. All Kane did was give a warning growl.

It was another thing Josh noticed. Kane hadn't been talking like he used to. Not a sound besides the growling slipped past his lips.

The moment Kane dropped to his knees, the staff moved. They opened the cage, dragging him to the cot. Josh walked in with the syringe in hand. He stuck Kane in the arm, his face expressionless while it took effect.

Jason motioned for the girl to be brought in as he walked over to Sasha's cage. Kane's eyes went with him, since he was too drugged to do anything else, and growled again when Jason's arm went around her neck, pulling her from the cage.

"Here's the deal, Kane," Josh said, getting those cold blue eyes to look at him. "You perform really nice with this girl here for me, including filling her up nicely or…" He snapped his fingers and Jason brought Sasha closer. "Jason will get to have some special time with your pretty little sister." He shrugged. "Your call."

Kane stared at Sasha. Jason was whispering things in her ear, and all color drained from her face. One of his hands grabbed her breast as he continued to talk to her quietly.

"You motherfucker," Kane growled, talking for the first time in months. "When I get out of here I'm going to rip your fucking throat out!" he yelled.

"Then, we are at an understanding." Josh motioned for the girl to be brought into the cage.

A guard closed the door the second the young woman was shoved into the cage. She was so drugged that she could only fall to the floor. Kane was weak from the drug Josh gave him, but he was hard. He got up from the cot, and on shaking legs, walked over to the female. He turned her away from him, took her by the neck and bent her over the cot, all the while watching Josh as he positioned his cock behind her.

Using his legs, he forced hers apart and, with a fluid motion, entered her body. Kane closed his eyes and did what he was supposed to, like a machine. There was no emotion in the act, no enjoyment. And Josh didn't miss a thing.

It only lasted a few minutes and then it was all over. Kane did as he was told and filled her up to the point that his seed was on her legs. He pushed away from her and stood at the far end of his cage, waiting for them to take her away.

Josh snapped his fingers and the guards went inside, taking the girl out. "Good boy," he said to Kane.

"Water, soap, towel," Kane ordered, his voice deep and his eyes narrowed on Josh.

"No please?" Josh raised an eyebrow. "And here I thought we taught you some kind of manners." Kane snarled. "Jason," Josh said. Please take our pet and clean him up. We don't want him stinking the place up."

"No problem." Jason shoved Sasha away from him and loaded the gun with another dart. He aimed and shot Kane in the chest. He went down quickly. "Take him downstairs."

Thirty minutes later Jason came into Josh's office with a smile on his face. Josh didn't have to ask if he enjoyed himself or not. He already knew the answer. Jason loved to use the powerful fire hose to clean Kane, and with the way the guards were dragging Kane in, he knew his cleaning had been very thorough.

"Well, your test worked, Jason," Josh sighed. "She didn't conceive which makes me confident that the drugs are doing their thing."

"Good. I'll get you another girl soon to make sure."

Josh laughed. "You can't keep taking these women from the street.

Someone is bound to notice them missing."

"Not the ones I'll bring you." Jason grinned in a cruel manner.

Josh shook his head and sat back in his chair. "We might have a winner here." Jason rubbed his hands together. "He might be sterile after all." Josh stood up. He walked to the edge of his office where he had a clear view of the two. "Get me a sperm sample. I want to make damn sure he is. Only then will we work up our plan to hit the others with it."

* * * *

Kane sat on his cot with his sore back resting on the bars of the cage, legs drawn up to his chest, arms resting over his knees and the only blanket he had across his groin. He welcomed the pain and fought off the exhaustion that threatened to knock him out. It had been a hell of a day, one he could have for sure lived without. He kept trying to think about different things. Anything that might help him to keep his mind off what his sister had to watch him do. His pride couldn't stand for her to see him being forced to do that to a girl. It was bad enough that he couldn't protect her or that they refused to let Sasha near him anymore, but for her to see him having to do that, whatever it was, was unbearable.

He was just about to nod off when his hearing picked up a faint clicking sound. Kane opened his eyes, shook the sleepiness away and looked around. He saw nothing in the darkness, but he could feel someone who wasn't part of the staff watching him.

Kane was about to shake it off as wishful thinking when he caught the scent of something that didn't belong in the lab. Something that was new and fresh. He looked around and sat up, sniffing.

The thing between his legs stiffened, and there wasn't a damn thing he could do to hide it, because he was a large man and naked except for the blanket on his lap.

His nose had caught that faint scent again of a female and for the first time ever in his life he wanted it. Kane wanted who ever it was that owned that scent, and he never wanted anyone near him but Sasha. But this was different from sibling nearness. So it was a strange feeling for him. One that he wasn't too sure about.

Kane closed his eyes and took as much of that sweet scent into his lungs as he could. And boy was it sweet. Different from Sasha's smell. Sasha had a softer scent to her, one that fit who she was. The one he picked up now seemed to have a different *feel* to it. Which was very strange. Kane would have sworn he could feel that scent just as he was smelling it. He grabbed onto the bars, dragging more and more in, and when his eyes opened, it went away almost as quickly as it had come.

He looked over at his sister. *Sasha?* Kane asked with his mind. *Sasha, answer me.* They discovered that it was the only thing they could do alike. He heard that bastard up there refer to him as a shifter or wolf, but didn't understand what it meant. They also said that Sasha had nothing. He didn't know what they were talking about. What he did know was that she was different from him and they could talk with their minds. He could see her dreams, and she saw his and, at night, they would come together in a special room to comfort each other.

Kane watched as she shook from the cold. They didn't give either one of them warm enough blankets but at least she got something to wear. Kane learned early on to block out the cold just like she had to learn to get used to seeing him naked.

It wasn't your fault. He tried again.

I feel your pain, she said tenderly. *You hurt.*

Kane smiled. *It will be all right. I can handle the pain. And the water got that one's scent off of me.*

That thing you have every month is different this time. Stronger.

Kane sighed and looked around the lab. *Yeah, it's stronger.*

I'm cold, Kane.

You hang in there. We are going to get out.

I don't want to watch them hurt you again. I don't want to see you doing that thing with those girls anymore!

Kane could feel her sorrow in his head. He felt her coldness and her worry. He knew the drugs were affecting him, not only physically, but chemically. Kane knew the bastard who had taken Sasha and him over, was trying to sterilize him. Slowly that plan was working. As long as he played by their rules though, he kept Sasha safe. But Kane was starting to notice the rules were changing. He was looking for the right moment when he could bust them both out and be free and he needed to do it soon. He didn't know how, but he had to before Jason raped his sister.

I'm so cold, Kane!

Just a little bit longer. I promise that soon you will not be cold any longer.

* * * *

Cole walked over to Chase's place around ten in the morning. Celine was still sleeping, Drake and Carrick went to town, so it was the perfect time for him to go over and make things right with his brother.

As much as Cole hated to admit it, his brother did good. The crazy plan of making Cole crazy with jealousy worked perfectly. If Chase hadn't done it then Cole might never have done the right thing and taken Celine to mate. Right before he headed over he made the call, making it all official. Celine Draeger was now Celine Sexton, Cole's mate. And damn if it didn't feel good.

"Hey Chase!" he yelled once he got closer to the camper. "Get your ass up!"

Cole banged on the back door and got no response. He went around the front and frowned when he saw a letter taped to the door with his name on it. Pulling it off and ripping it open he read it.

Cole,

Glad things are working out between you and Celine. She is perfect for you. I've taken off to go look for Jada. She hasn't called me like she promised, and I haven't heard from her for several days. That isn't good. So don't worry, I'll be fine. You just take care of that hot woman of yours or the next time I step in I'll take her for real.

I'll call in a couple of days. Try not to worry, 'Dad'.

Chase.

"Well shit." Cole fisted the letter in his hand. Chase going out there to look for Jada, who was more than likely in some serious trouble wasn't good. And the night before the full moon. Not good!

He turned and headed right back to Drake's. When he walked in the front door, his nose picked up the mouth-watering scent of food. His stomach growled and his feet took him right to the kitchen.

Celine and Carrick were busy cooking breakfast and Drake was at the table reading the file that Chase had given him. The information Jada had discovered.

"Chase left," he said, taking a seat. "Went after Jada."

Everyone stopped and stared at him. Both of Drake's eyebrows went up. He was clearly surprised.

"Why would he do that?" Celine asked.

"I don't know." Cole sighed, rubbing his chin. "Left me a letter saying she hasn't checked in with him for a few days. Guess that is unusual for her."

"What do you know about this Jada person?" Drake asked. "I mean, its not like we all don't have human friends who know our secret, but I just got the impression the first time I saw her that she's trouble."

Cole snickered, "Oh she can be a pill that's for sure. But you want her on your side." Celine handed him a plate of food and he smiled at her. "Thanks."

"How long have you guys known her? Carrick asked.

Cole shrugged, "Chase has known her longer than me. Doesn't have any family, she used to spend the holidays at school alone. A couple times at Christmas Chase stayed with her until Natasha had him bring her home for the holidays." He took a bite of his eggs, chewing quickly before he went on. "She mostly kept to Chase. Guess she didn't trust me."

"But she knows about you guys?" Carrick asked with a wave of her hand back and forth between him and Drake.

"Yeah, Chase said she figured it out one month when he was having a very bad month. If you know what I mean?"

"And they never—" Celine started to say, but Cole cut her off.

"No! I already asked him that." Cole chuckled.

"What I don't understand is how she could find all this stuff out when we couldn't," Carrick started, taking the file from Drake. "I mean, I lived with the man and couldn't get this kind of information."

"Guess you'll just have to ask her when you see her." Drake took the file back and Cole stared opened mouth at him with his fork half way to it.

"Huh?" Cole said.

"I want her here," Drake placed his finger on the table, a frown of determination across his face. "I want to know everything she knows."

Cole lowered his fork back down to his plate. "That isn't going to be so easy, Drake. She's tight lipped about everything! Your grandmother couldn't get information out of her, what makes you think you can?"

"Yeah, you didn't do too well with me either," Carrick cocked her head at him and smiled. "On the information getting part," she breathed out sweetly.

Celine chuckled softly and Cole had to hide his smile behind his hand.

"Anyway," Drake went on, giving Cole his full attention again. "I'm sure she knows more about these two and we need to know it."

"You've got a plan," Celine pointed her finger at him.

Drake nodded and pushed away from the table. "Yep. Going to go in there and get them."

"Now I know for a fact you are suicidal!" Carrick raised her voice and Cole took this as a hint it was time to leave.

He grabbed Celine's hand, pulling her from the table and out of the kitchen just in time. Drake and Carrick started arguing.

"Come on, we'll go to town for breakfast," he said.

The drive was pleasant. Cole couldn't stop glancing over at Celine who was smiling with her head back on the seat, sun shining in her face. She's so damn beautiful. And it was hard for him to believe that finally she was his.

"I made the call this morning," he said, getting her full attention. Cole reached over, touching her leg. Today she was dressed in a simple pair of jean shorts and t-shirt. He rubbed her leg. "You are officially Celine Sexton."

She leaned over and kissed him on the cheek, "I've been that since I was twelve."

Town was small. The main street had a few small shops and many more empty buildings. There was one that caught his attention right off. An old brick building at the end of the street.

There were two diners, craft store, general mill, food store, small camping and hunting store, hotel and a few others. But what they didn't have was a construction shop. How did anyone build a home if they didn't have one?

They went into the closest diner, sat down, and ordered a huge breakfast. One thing about Celine, she could eat with the best of them, but not one ounce of it landed on her body. It was her shifter side that had her eating like one of them. Natasha said it was the only thing shifter Celine received from her father. She was all human but for her appetite.

"You think Chase will find her?" Celine asked with a mouth full of food.

Cole laughed, wiped his mouth before picking up his glass of juice. "Want to wait until you finish eating?"

She smiled, swallowed, and wiped her mouth also. "Sorry."

"And yes. I know Chase will find her. The only thing worrying me is what happens after he does."

"What do you mean?"

Cole took a deep breath and sat back in his seat, letting it out slowly. "I don't know Jada as well as Chase does, but I do know she doesn't follow anyone's rules but her own. Drake is going to make a big mistake if he brings her out here. First she'll go nuts then drive us all with her."

Celine smiled, shook her head and picked up her toast, "You make her sound terrible."

"She's not terrible. Jada is actually a lot of fun once you get to know her. But she's distant. Doesn't get too close to anyone or stay in one place for too long. So yeah, Chase will find her, it's just a matter of how long is it going to take."

"Any ideas on what you think she found out?"

"No clue, and right now I don't want to think about it." He picked up her hand, and kissed it. "Eat up. I want to take a look at the town."

He paid the bill, took her hand, and left the little diner, to walk down the street. There were many different store fronts which were empty. It almost looked like the town was dying.

"This place is great, but needs some life to it." Cole stated, looking into one of the closed stores.

"Needs a bakery," Celine stated.

Cole got this strange idea in his head and spoke up. "Why don't you?"

Celine turned from the dirty window with her mouth open. "What?"

"Yeah, you and Carrick can cook damn good. Don't see why not. It's a great idea, and it ought to bring some life back to the place."

"You're out of your mind," she laughed, walking away. But she didn't go too far. Celine stopped and turned back around. "But sometimes the craziest ideas are the best."

He went up to her, draping his arm over her shoulders, "Now you're talking."

They went over to the end of the street where the brick building stood. There was a for sale sign in the broken, dirty window. An old sign hung over the door. Around the back, there was a docking platform for trucks to bring in goods. Deceiving from the front, it was a two story building.

Cole was in love with the place, only he didn't know what in the world he could do with it.

* * * *

"It's a great idea!" Celine whined to Drake at dinner. "I can bake anything."

"Yeah, but what do you know about running a business?" Drake pointed his finger at her and Carrick slapped him on the shoulder.

"Give her a break," Carrick said. "I think it's a good idea too. Why can't she try to start a bakery in this town? Have you looked around the place? It needs life Drake or it's going to die."

"Your dad wants you to finish school," Drake went on, ignoring Carrick. "How are you going to do both."

"I'm going to do it with her," Carrick told her over his shoulder.

"No way!" Drake yelled.

Celine rolled her eyes at him, slumped back in her seat with her arms crossed over her chest. "Now you sound like a damn bigot."

"Hey!" Drake frowned at Celine.

"Come on, Drake. You like Carrick home, like the obedient mate."

"No I like her safe and with her damn nutty father out there the woods here are perfect to keep her that way."

"Stop being a damn bear," Cole came into the kitchen, cell phone in hand. He grabbed a chair, turned it around, and straddled the seat, tossing the phone on the table. "Start thinking with your stomach, man. All that pastry, cakes, cookies, breads. Mmmm, damn it makes me hungry just thinking about it."

"Not helping here," Drake grumbled.

"No luck getting a hold of Chase?" Carrick asked.

"Not answering," Cole sighed.

"Speaking of calling," Drake returned his attention back to Celine. "Have you called your father yet to let him know how things are going between you two?"

"No. I was going to call home in a bit." Celine pointed her finger at him, "And I bet he will support my idea." Cole snickered and Celine got up, taking his phone, leaving the room. She dialed the number as she headed for the porch. "Hi mom!"

"Hey baby! How're things going?" Jaclyn asked.

Celine smiled, "He did it! He claimed me!" She couldn't keep from smiling or sounding like an excited child. "God, I never thought it would be this good."

"We got the call this morning about the claim. Your dad is grumbling, but happy Cole did the right thing. How is everything else up there?"

"Not too bad. Chase set up a camper on the ground grandma gave him to live on. So he sort of moved out of the house. Mom, um, I want to do something but don't know how you guys will feel about it. Drake hates the idea."

"Since when has he ever hated anything you do?" Jaclyn laughed.

"Since I want to start a bakery business." Celine bit her lower lip when it got quiet on the phone. "Mom?"

"Wow, Celine, that's a lot of work you're talking about. Are you sure you want to do something like that?"

"This place is so beautiful and the town needs so much help. I think opening a bakery will really help it."

"But what about school?" Jaclyn sighed. "You know your father wants you to finish college."

"And I will!" she rushed on. "I'll change my major to business. That'll give me the time I need to get the place fixed up. Carrick is thinking about working with me, as soon as she can convince Drake."

"You really are going to have to talk this over with your father, Celine. I'm all for making your way in this world, but your dad is old fashioned. He's very protective of the family. He might not think it's such a great idea with Stan out there trying to kill everyone."

Celine ran her hand through her hair, sitting down on the steps. "I understand that, but I also need a life. We all need a life and we can't keep hiding because of that lunatic!"

"Celine you aren't telling me anything I don't already know." Jaclyn sighed. "Tell you what. I do think having something you can call your own is great. So on one condition will I talk to your father for you. Make that two."

She was almost afraid to ask. "What?"

"One. You have to finish school. There is no way in hell your father will even consider saying yes if you drop out."

"And the other?"

"Have to bribe your mother monthly with those damn sticky buns of yours."

Celine smiled. "I think I can handle that."

"I'll see what I can do, but I make no promises, you know he only wants what's best for you." Jaclyn wasn't joking anymore on the other end. "He might not even okay a thing until after you finish school."

"Well, tell him that at the end of summer I'll be home to finish school, only if he okays this."

Jaclyn laughed, "You are just like him."

"That's funny, Drake says I'm just like you!" Celine giggled. "Night. Tell Daddy I love him and will call back soon."

"Take care, you know we love you , baby."

"Love you too, mom."

"Well, what'd he say?"

Celine jumped. Cole had snuck outside, scaring her. "Damn-it, Cole!"

Cole laughed, "Sorry."

"He wasn't there, talked to my mother." She stood up, handing him the phone. "My mother likes the idea and is going to work on him for me. But part of the deal is I have to finish school if I want to do anything."

"I agree," he nodded, sliding his hands into his pockets. "You should finish school. It's very important."

"But what about this?"

Cole reached for her and Celine went very willingly into his arms. "What we have will never go away. You go where I go, and I go where you go. It's that simple. You go back to school; I'll be there with you. You're not going to lose me Celine. You're stuck with me for life now."

She smiled, reached up, touching his face. "You really are the best, you know that."

"Well I do try," he winked.

"So, the full moon is tomorrow night."

"Uh-huh," he nodded, swaying back and forth with her.

"Want to give me a hint as to what I can expect?"

"Umm, not really."

Celine squealed and hit him in the arm. "That's not fair!"

"I know." He had a wicked glint in his eye. "But you need to have something to look forward to."

She raised her chin and played with his long hair, "Can I look forward to something tonight, instead?"

"Oh," he chuckled. "You little devil." He kissed her on the tip of the nose. "And the answer is no. You have to wait for *that* until tomorrow night."

"Payback is a bitch Cole, you do know that."

He kissed her deep, stealing her breath, "Umm, I look forward to it." He moaned against her lips. "Now get your sweet ass up to bed. You're going to need all the rest you can get because I intend to keep you up very late tomorrow night."

"You're a damn tease, you know that?"

"Learned over the years at your heels, baby." He kissed her again. "Now go!" he turned, gave her a slight shove to the door with a swat on her ass.

"God, this better be worth it."

Chapter Seven

Celine soaked in the tub, making sure every spot on her body was clean and shaved. She spent almost an hour in her room trying to decide what to wear or not wear for Cole's night. She settled for something very simple. Thong and robe.

Taking a quick peek at the full moon, Celine smiled, took a deep breath, and left her room for Cole's. The house was quiet. Carrick decided since it was Celine's first heat with Cole that she would let the two of them have the house to themselves and she'd take Drake out into the woods. Drake was more than happy to go out there with her. Celine heard him say something about chasing her down.

As quietly as she could, Celine opened Cole's door and slipped inside. He pounced on her before the door closed. He pushed her over to the bed, forcing her to bend over. Then without saying a word, he yanked her robe from her body and the thong, with a rip, followed.

He was hot, solid muscle with hair teasing her legs, rear, and back. When she was able to get a quick glimpse of him, she wasn't shocked at what she saw.

Cole had changed just slight, his eyes deep and red. Soft hair was all over his naked body. She groaned at the feel of this thick cock pressing against the cheeks of her ass. Just being pinned between the bed and him had her pussy weeping for attention and her nipples throbbing. He was in the form she had always dreamed him to be, and Celine could barely wait for him to take her hard.

"Are you ready for this?" His voice had a rumble to it when he spoke, almost like it was purring but with a growl. "Are you ready to play my way?"

Celine answered him with a nod of her head.

"Is little CeeCee ready for the wolf?" His hands went up to her breasts and he squeezed them hard enough for her to feel a new kind of throb between her legs. "I'm going to eat your sweet pussy." Cole pulled at her nipples and she groaned, rubbing her ass back against him. "I'm going to lick all the cream that you have to give and fuck that snug little cunt of yours with my tongue." Cole growled low. "And *only* when you think you can't take it will I give you my dick."

His hands squeezed at her breasts, pulling on her nipples until she knew she was going to die from the pleasure and pain. In fact, Celine wasn't sure if she could handle the whole thing if she got this kind of pleasure just from his hands on her breasts.

"Have you ever been spanked?" he asked, which had her whimpering in need. "Does that thought get you wet for me?"

She had no shame at the moment only a burning need. Celine hung her head down and sighed, "Yes!"

Cole chuckled. "First things first." He fisted his hand into her hair, pulling her back against him. "On your knees, Celine. I want to fuck your mouth before I ease into your pussy."

She turned and dropped to her knees. Without any hesitation, she took hold of his straining flesh, opened her mouth, and took as much as she could into her mouth. She moaned against him, getting a deep growl and moan from him in return.

Celine relaxed her throat and let Cole fuck her mouth like he wanted. She sucked hard, pulling on his flesh when he pulled out. The pain on her head from him pulling at her hair seemed to heighten the throbbing of her clit. If at any time she had needed to be fucked, and fucked raw, this was it.

She got no warning at all. Cole pushed his whole length down her throat, head back and he came with a deep vibrating growl. She drank it all, loving his taste, wanting more.

But Cole wasn't going to give her more. He pulled his cock from her mouth quickly, took her arm, and got her back up on her feet only to push her down on his bed. On purpose, she scooted to the center and parted her legs, showing him a freshly shaved pussy just for him.

"Ohhh," he chuckled deep, crawling on the bed at her feet, "Are you trying to tease and tempt me?"

She was breathing hard from the excitement, her nipples painful hard points, her clit in more need then she'd ever felt. "Maybe," she huffed in barely a whisper.

With the small amount of fur over his body, the red eyes, and thick cock, Celine had the sudden urge to rub herself up against him. He gave her a grin, and it sent chills down her spine. It wasn't an evil grin, but it wasn't one that was all fun and games either. Cole was in heat, and her body was his cure.

She was helpless as he went down on his elbows, parted her legs further, and took one long slow inhale. He growled low and it caused her to shiver. Celine couldn't watch him, hell she could barely control the shaking of her body, and almost lost control just from his touching her with his tongue.

His tongue was wet and had a rough feeling to it, thanks to his slight change. He pressed against her clit and she sucked air into her lungs. Celine didn't think she was going to be able to stand still and let him just feast upon her, but she sure as hell was going to give it a good try.

Fingers parted the lips and he licked her from her ass all the way to her stiff clit. Celine raised her hips up to meet him and tried to get his tongue to linger longer on her clit. It felt so good to have him touch her there that she didn't want it to end, she was very close to an orgasm.

Cole flicked the tip of his tongue so fast, teased the nub that was throbbing between her legs that Celine just knew she was going to pass out with her need.

He purred against her and she almost came. "You taste heavenly."

"You're killing me Cole," she panted back. "I don't think I can handle this."

His tongue pushed inside her and she lost it. Celine cried out. Her orgasm hit and she was powerless to push it back or hold off.

It seemed that it was only the tip of what Cole had in store for her.

She was still enjoying and coming down from that pleasure when she felt his fingers tease not only her clit but also the small puckered opening of her ass. She was so thankful that he had her on the bed and wasn't trying this shit standing up. She would be on the floor in a heartbeat.

His mouth closed over her clit, sucking it hard, and one finger went into her pussy and another into her ass. Celine couldn't help herself and screamed. He fucked her with his fingers and sucked hard on her clit, pushing her to another mind-blowing climax.

"Cole, Cole, Cole," she gasped his name, grabbing the headboard tightly until her knuckles turned white. "Cole!" Celine screamed his name and came again.

Instead of begging him to stop, Cole seemed to know that she couldn't handle this any longer. Before she was completely down from her high, he grabbed her hips, flipped her over onto her stomach, legs pushed further apart, and a hairy body up against her backside.

She had time enough to take only two deep breaths before he shoved every thick inch inside her.

He was thick, stretching her to a burning pleasure and pain. Celine didn't think she was going to be able to breathe but somehow she did. Cole moved behind her almost brutally. He thrust hard and fast into her, slamming her with everything he had. She could only hold onto the bedding and take what he had to give, loving every second of it.

"Can you handle it?" Cole asked, his voice raspy and thick. "Can you handle what I have to give tonight?"

"I, I, I," she could barely think with his pounding behind her. In fact it took all of her concentration to keep herself in the position he'd placed her in. "I can take it," she breathed out. "Anything you've got."

He stopped and ground as well as rotated his hips, cock buried to the hilt inside her. The movement made her groan. It felt like he was going to rip her in two, he was so thick and long

"Is that so?" She held her breath and closed her eyes the moment his hand went between her legs. "Then let's see how you handle this."

He moved again, only this time he fucked her so hard that she bumped into his hand between her legs. Cole teased, flicked, and pinched her clit until she was seeing stars behind her eyes. Raw, blinding pleasure gripped her and only increased the tempo to go with his thrusts. Celine was powerless to do anything more than hang on and ride it out, praying that she would get that orgasm soon. But when he slapped her between the legs she could do nothing but cry out from the pleasure.

"Later on I'll show you what a real spanking to you will do," he said in her ear.

He left her pussy to part the globes of her rear and one finger forced its way into her ass as far as it could go. That pushed her over the edge. Celine screamed and shook with the climax, and still Cole plunged into her.

"Fuck, Celine," he groaned. "Your pussy clamps down so hard on my dick I have to use all my willpower to hold back and not come right now." He slammed harder into her and all Celine could do was shake her head and wait for the next one to come. "I'm close, baby," he purred in her ear. "Are you ready for a hard fuck in your ass?"

Her answer was to cry out and push back against him, another orgasm hitting her. The finger in her ass moved just as fast as his cock, and the other hand moved juices back. Somehow, Cole prepared her ass and still fucked her.

Cole stopped without any warning, pulled out of her body. She breathed hard, resting her forehead on the cool sheets while Cole took more of her juices and release, smearing it back pushing it into her ass, lubing her up.

She shook each time a finger or two pushed inside her rear, anticipation killing her while he prepared her for his final entry. The moment she felt the hot head butt against her, she held her breath waiting for it.

Cole grabbed hold of the checks, parted them, and with growing determination, she felt the push. A whimper left her lips when the small ring gave, and she bit her lip at the burn she felt. Celine knew deep down Cole was trying to be somewhat gentle with her in this position, she only wondered how long that gentleness was going to last.

It didn't last very long. She would guess that he was only a quarter of the way in before he shoved the whole length into her. Celine screamed and started to cry, not from pain but from the pressure and throbbing between her legs.

He rode her just as hard and fast as he'd taken her pussy. Celine cried out with each thrust, each pound he gave, but she also begged him for more. She urged him on by pushing back against him. Cole growled and snarled. He even gave her breasts and nipples a few pulls and squeezes before moving his hand between her legs and shoving two fingers into her. She was fucked by both ends, so to speak, and it was slowly driving her crazy.

Her body felt like it was going in a direction that she could no longer control. She could feel the orgasm, but it was so far out of her reach that she knew she was never going to get it. That frustrated and just plain pissed her off to the point that she was crying actual tears.

It wasn't until she was about to scream out to do it harder that she understood what it was that she really needed. It wasn't him being brutal and relentless, but it was the bite she needed. She had to have Cole on the edge, the beast out to claim her that would make this all complete. She needed the animal!

"Damn you, Cole," she sniffed back the tears.

Cole chuckled, "Want something?" He sounded innocent and rough, but she knew he was anything *but* innocent at the moment.

"Yeah, stop being a pussy and finish this!"

She heard the snarl, felt more hair sprout on his body and he pulled her hair to the side, bringing out a hiss of pain from her lips. But the bite didn't come. Instead, he licked her shoulder and sucked on the mark he left days ago.

"You're almost there," he said in her ear. "Almost, but not quite."

He pulled her head back, kept teasing her shoulder, and kept fucking her ass with everything he had now. She burned back there, and loved every painful inch of it. Celine wanted to remember this night for a few days. She wanted the aches and pains that went along with a heat night, and she was definitely getting her wish.

So Celine decided to try a different tactic. Bait and snatch.

She laughed, "It figures. You can't do it. You wait all this time to get me on a full moon and you hold back on me." She turned her head, meeting his red eyes.

And that did it.

His face changed some, taking on more of his animal and his mouth opened. She closed her eyes and welcomed the pain of the bite, relishing the pleasure of the most powerful orgasm she ever had in her life.

Celine reached over her head, fisted both hands into his hair and reared up. She sat down on him, his cock shoved more into her and expanded. She felt his climax and pulled on his hair, grinding on top of him even more. Cole growled against her shoulder and both hands came around her, cupping her breasts, squeezing them.

She didn't know how long they stayed like that. She felt the hair on his body slowly go away, felt him shift and his cock leave her body.

"Thank you," Cole sighed when he released her shoulder, resting instead his forehead against her.

Celine smiled and rested her head back on his shoulder. "Now what?"

He took a deep breath, but didn't move. "Now we get some sleep. I'm damn tired."

* * * *

Celine was tired and sore, but couldn't sleep. She lay in his arms, head resting on his chest, hand sliding back and forth over his stomach. His body was still hot, warming her enough so she didn't need the sheet or blankets.

"You should be sleeping," Cole said, his voice groggy.

Celine grinned, "So should you."

"What's wrong?"

She took a deep breath, snuggling closer. "How'd you do it for so long?"

"Do what?"

"Act like nothing was wrong when you came to the house or when ever I was around." She raised up, resting her head on her hand. "How did you put on such an act as though I didn't mean anything to you?"

"It wasn't easy," he sighed, his eyes closed. "The only thing I could think of was to stay as far away from you as I could get, or get killed by your father."

"And that worked?"

He slowly inhaled, letting it out with a shake of his head. "No. Not really." He chuckled. He opened his eyes, looking down at her. "It killed me every time your grandmother dragged me to the house and I had to see you, smell you, and know that I couldn't touch you. It was pure torture."

"Why didn't you tell me though," she sighed, resting her chin on his chest. "I could've helped."

Cole reached out took a strand of her hair and wrapped it around his finger. "You were still too young. You needed the time to grow up."

"But you still could've told me." She punched him lightly in the stomach, causing him to grunt.

He hugged her tight. "I guess I could have." Celine raised back up, one eyebrow going up. Cole shrugged and looked very guilty. "I just didn't want the family to know." She was about to hit him again, but he stopped her by grabbing hold of her wrist. "Hey, your father is a bit scary now. I heard he almost broke a guy in half with his bare hands."

Celine laughed, "He didn't do that, Uncle Adrian did. Dad helped blow the building up."

"Still, it's very nerve racking being around him." Cole shivered. "He's a big man."

Celine snuggled back down, but she still couldn't close her eyes. "You know that Uncle Stefan knew when Aunt Sidney was young, *and* he told her."

"Yes, but he also didn't have a beast, correction, an over protective beast breathing down any male's neck that might come sniffing for his little girl."

She couldn't stop from giggling at the thought. Cole was right, however. If he came around when he first knew and told Dedrick, then he would more than likely have the shit beat out of him. It was a thing that all males of their race had about protecting their females to the death. None of them liked to give a daughter up and did just about everything they could to prevent a claiming that they didn't like.

Dedrick had been trying for years now to get the Counsel to change the way it did a gathering. He now had two nieces, and like their father, didn't want to see them being forced to a gathering and taken from Adrian. He wanted to modernize it. Make it so that if a male was interested and met his mate at a gathering, then he had to date and get to know the family, earn their trust, respect and honor from the father, before he could claim and take his mate. The counsel didn't want that. They wanted to keep it the way it was now. A female goes to a gathering, if claimed, then she is taken away from her family—a Barbaric custom.

"Okay, so you have a point," she said. "But my point is this. If you would have told me then, I could have helped you with my father. Softened him up a bit."

Cole took a deep breath, letting it out slowly, then yawned. "Okay, the next time I have to approach your father I'll let you do it for me. Now go to sleep."

She smiled, kissed his chest, and hooked a leg over his, "I don't think I've ever been this drained before, and I love it. Promise me that you'll be like this every full moon?"

"Oh I won't promise, just guarantee it."

* * * *

Chase was hunched down on his hands and knees, naked, gasping, sweaty and in major pain. It was over, but not only did it hurt worse than before, it also left him so weak he couldn't stand up, only drop face first to the floor.

"Fuck I hate this," he moaned in pain.

Chase was glad he was away from Cole this month. He felt like something was changing inside him, something he couldn't explain.

His phone rang. What little strength he had, Chase dragged himself over to the small table where he left it. He wrapped his hands around it and rolled over to his back, breathing hard. The ID showed it was Jada, finally.

"Where the hell are you?"

"Well hello to you to," Jada laughed. "Are we having a bad night?" Chase growled. "I'll take that as a yes. You rang?"

"Jada, I need to know where you're at?" He wanted to sit up, but couldn't.

"Chase," she sighed, "It's on a need to know basis, and at the moment you really don't need to know."

"Yes, I do," he stated through his teeth.

"Why are you out there? I know you checked in that little motel off of sixty-seven. And I know you got my text stating to stay the hell away."

Yeah, he got her message. *Don't come. Too dangerous.* That right there was the red flag telling him to go look for her sorry ass. Listening to his gut was the smartest thing, and that message only confirmed it all.

He wrote up his own message and sent it to her. *We are going to meet tomorrow night. No excuses.* But a response back didn't come, and that pissed him off. He knew Jada well enough to know that she didn't like being told what to do, but this time it was different. This time she was in way over her head and needed to get out before she drowned in this war.

"Why are *you* still snooping around when I told you it was too damn dangerous?" he snapped back. "They'll kill you if they find you!"

"Ahh, they have to catch me first." She giggled.

"Dammit, Jada!" His anger gave him the strength he needed to get up off the floor. He swayed a bit to the bed and dropped down heavily to the edge. "This isn't a fucking game. Those bastards will kill anything and anyone that discovers their secrets."

"Chase I know what I'm doing." He opened his mouth to tell her she didn't, but didn't get a chance. The line went dead. She'd hung up on him. "Dammit!" he growled loudly.

He dropped back on the bed, letting the phone fall to the floor. Chase fisted both hands in his hair in frustration. Fuck she could piss him off like no other person ever had. Jada was one of the most stubborn humans he had ever met in his life!

"I swear when I get my hands on you I'm going to kill you myself," he mumbled to himself.

Chapter Eight

Jada Leonard walked through a dark neighborhood toward the all night café where she'd been going for the past few nights for dinner. She kept looking over her shoulder. She had this feeling as if she was being followed or watched. It was spooky out tonight. It was foggy which only added to the creepiness of the night. She couldn't shake the chills off or the being watched feeling.

In her possession, she had a fresh set of photos that she needed to stash with the other stuff she had. A nice little collection that she would send to Chase right before she disappeared. It hadn't been easy to get this latest batch of information, so this time she did a backup of everything in case she was caught. She put everything she had on a flash drive and hid it where no one would ever think to look, along with a little something else she was planning on taking. It was her insurance just in case things got too sticky for her and she needed a way out. The way she was feeling now, she might just take it.

Jada turned the corner and someone grabbed her and pulled her deep into the shadows. She opened her mouth to scream, but a hand closed over her mouth before she could make a sound.

"Shhh, it's me," Chase whispered, easing his hand from her mouth. "I'm being followed so keep your damn mouth shut."

"Dammit Chase!" She hit him in the chest, trying to keep her voice down. "You scared the shit out of me."

He pressed his hand to her mouth, then jerked his head to the left so she would look behind him. Jada took a peek over his shoulder and saw a of couple guys in leather jackets trying to act casual but they were sticking out like a sore thumb. "Fuck," she sighed. "You just had to bring a tail with you, didn't ya?"

Before anything else could be said he pushed her farther into the darkness and her mouth went dry when two more guys passed by. So, she was being followed after all.

"They've picked up on your shit also. Did you get caught?" he asked.

"No!" She kept her voice low and pulled away from Chase. "I told you to stay away. And that I'd send you the stuff. You didn't have to come out here." She shoved the small pictures at him. "Here. They're trying to breed him or some shit." Chase flipped through the photos in the dark as best as he could. "He's different from you, Chase." That caught his attention and he stopped to look at her. "Senses are sharper, he's stronger. I...I don't know how the hell they are keeping him controlled like they are, but something…I…"

"You've seen too damn much Jada," He put the pictures inside his jacket and took hold of her arm, dragging her into the alley. "Now its time for you to stop and get the hell out."

"The hell I am!" she said, trying to get her arm free. "I know who the hell his father is Chase."

Chase stopped and pushed her up against a brick wall. "What?"

"You heard me." She was breathing hard when she looked up at him. "I know who Kane's father is."

"Tell me."

"Fuck no." She shook her head, pushing at him. Jada might as well try to move a brick wall. "If I give you that I'm screwed."

"This isn't a damn game here, Jada," Chase said through his teeth, shaking her.

"No shit." She tried to twist out of his hold, but couldn't get out.

"What the hell am I going to do?" he whispered.

Jada opened her mouth to tell him what he could do and where he could go, but didn't get the chance.

"Down here!" someone yelled.

"Let's go!" Chase grabbed her hand and started running. Someone fired a gun at them and she screamed, ducking as best as she could since she was being dragged along. "Get on!" he told her when they stopped next to a motorcycle.

"Don't have to tell me twice."

Jada swung her leg over the side wrapped her arms tightly around his waist and closed her eyes when he took off. But the ride was a short one.

Gunfire brought the bike to a very rough stop. The back tire had been shot, Chase turned so they were headed for some ground, and barely made it before he lost control and the bike went down to its side. She screamed before she hit the ground, sliding on the grass then rolling down a hill to stop hard at the bottom.

"Oh I'm going to have a bruise," she groaned under her breath, waiting to see if anything might be broken. "Better make that a few."

"Jada!" Chase yelled some ways away. She didn't move, not even when he came up to her, or more like dropped with a slide next to her. "You okay?"

"No, I'm dead." She opened her eyes and he smiled. "That's going to leave one hell of a mark on my backside."

"We need to get moving."

"You suck. You know that right?" she groaned before sitting up and hissing at the pain.

"So you've told me," he grabbed her hand, yanking her back to her feet fast. Jada moaned in pain. Damn she hurt everywhere.

Off in the distance sirens could be blared. Someone didn't waste any time in calling the cops for a shooting, but that didn't matter to her. What mattered was getting the hell out of here as fast as she could. The information she had was worth killing for, and Jada sort of liked life at the moment.

"Use this." Chase shoved a handgun in her hand. "We've got trouble."

"Chase I have a bad tendency when it comes to guns," she told him with a shrug, staring down at it. "Call it getting trigger happy sometimes."

He glared at her, one that said simply to shut up.

The four men who were following them were now running towards them. Chase pushed her behind him and took aim with another gun. She shot once, but the others also shot back. Chase was hit twice before he fell back, knocking Jada to the ground. His gun fell from his hand.

"Get the girl," one said.

Jada squeezed her hand on the gun, extended her hand out right in front of her, taking aim at the one who'd spoken. "Not today."

She pulled the trigger, hitting him right in the chest. Not giving it much thought she started firing at the others, hitting one in the arm and another in the leg. The one who hadn't been hit turned and ran.

She was breathing hard, shaking. Jada didn't know what to do next. Shock it seemed was gripping her.

"Jada." She jumped when she heard her name, swinging the gun and pointing it at the sound. "Easy. It's me. Chase."

She swallowed hard. Chase? No, he was shot. *They* shot him. "No." She shook her head and cocked the gun.

The gun was taken from her hand so fast she didn't even blink. Jada went into her fight mode. She kicked, swung wildly at whomever it was who'd taken her gun and tried to scoot away.

"Calm down!" Hard hands grabbed her legs and she was pulled close to a big, male body. She screamed, scared of what they were going to do to her now that they had their hands on her. "Shh!" A hand covered her mouth, muffling her screams. "Shh, it's me. Chase. You're all right."

It took her a few minutes, but Jada was able to finally focus her eyes on him. When he slowly took his hand from her mouth, she took in big gulps of air before touching his face. "They shot you," she breathed out.

"I know." Chase was breathing hard and clearly in pain. Jada shook herself out of her shock to sit up and look at his wounds. He had one in his thigh and another in his side that looked like it went right through.

"Shit, Chase," she groaned, "You're bleeding a lot."

"I need…shit…," he panted. "I need to get out of here and…take care of this."

She stood up, bent over and tried like hell to help him stand up. Where he got the strength to hold her down while she had her little panic attack, she didn't know. Because at the moment Chase was dead weight that she couldn't carry.

He fell, taking her with him. "Dammit, Chase!" Jada looked around and saw a black car with the doors open. She narrowed her eyes on it, one eyebrow going up with a plan. "Stay here."

She ran to the car, looked inside, and smiled when she saw the keys in it. Jada closed the back, got behind the wheel, started it and did a U-turn. She skidded to a stop on the side of the road where she'd left Chase.

"Get in!" she yelled, opening the passenger's door for him.

Chase crawled a bit before standing up and dashing for the car. Before his whole body was inside, she was flooring it, speeding away as fast as she could.

"Where're you going?" Chase panted.

"Away from here!" She glanced over at him. "Jesus, Chase. You're bleeding real bad."

"Co—copper," he stuttered. "Na—nasty shit."

"What?" she squealed out, taking a sharp right and praying like hell there wasn't a cop close.

"Co…copper," he stuttered again, his face getting very pale. "And…we are allergic to…it."

"One of these days you're going to have to finish explaining things to me." She told him, shaking her head while she looked for a place.

"Yeah, bu—but not right no—now." His whole body was shaking as if he had a fever.

"There's a place…" She turned off the road into a small motel. "Stay low and I'll be right back." Jada parked the car so the manager couldn't see Chase slumped in the front seat. With a smile on her face, she went inside. "Hi. I need a room please."

The guy looked her over, giving her the creeps. He licked his lips and rubbed his jaw. "Single or double?"

"Single," she answered, digging into her pocket, bringing out a hundred dollar bill. "One in the back where me and my boyfriend won't be disturbed." She winked. "He's a screamer you know?" He smiled, reached behind him for the last key on the hook. Jada snatched the key and wiggled the money in his face, but held onto it when he grabbed it. "And we won't be needing a wake-up call either."

"Whatever you want."

"You're a doll," she smiled, leaving the office with a bit of a sway to her ass.

Jada drove to the back of the motel. Chase had passed out. She had to slap him a couple of times on the face to wake him up enough to help her get him into the room.

"What the hell do you guys eat," she grunted as she helped him to the bed. "You weigh a damn ton."

Chase had his eyes closed, shaking. He didn't answer her, which was fine for the moment. She touched his forehead and frowned. "You're burning up."

Chase turned his head towards her and opened his eyes. They were glazed over, wild looking, appearing like he was in a daze, "Tape...tape it up," he gasped. "Stop the bleeding any...any way you...can."

"God you are soooooooo going to owe me," she sighed, looking around for something to use.

"Not this time." He shook each time he spoke and even tried to smile at her. "Now you...owe me."

"Put it on my tab." She found a small first aid kit in the bathroom. It was old, but was going to have to do at the moment. She also found some alcohol poured some it on his side. Chase yelled. Jada was a little shocked that his body was steaming from the liquid she poured over it. "I guess now would be a bad time to tell you that you have a nice body?"

Chase laughed and shook, "Very...bad time."

"Thought so." She put some gauze on the front and back wound on his side, then taped it up before she went to his leg. "Almost a distraction you know," she chuckled. "Think it should be a sin having a body like this. Do all of you look like this?" she groaned when she ripped his jeans, exposing the bullet hole in his leg. "Shit, Chase. Let's call your brother. I've...I've got a bad feeling about this."

He shook his head. "No. No, Cole."

"He's going to kill us both, you know that, right?"

Chase shook his head. When he spoke, his teeth seemed to rattle. "Don't worry about him."

"Sure, it's not your ass on the line here." She poured alcohol on his leg and Chase once more yelled. "Okay, I'll do this your way for now, but if you get worse I'm calling him and I don't give a damn what you say."

Shifters 5: Cole's Awakening

Chase nodded his agreement and she covered him up with a blanket once she was finished with his leg. She was worried. There was no exit wound on the leg, which meant the bullet was still in there. And if it was the kind he said it was, then she knew she was going to have to call Cole real soon to get it out.

* * * *

Celine rolled over to her stomach, reaching out for Cole and she came awake instantly when she didn't feel him. The bed was empty, the sun was shining brightly in the room, and water was running in the bathroom. With relief, she smiled and looked around for something to put on.

Her shoulder was sore, as was between her legs and her ass, but she didn't mind. In fact, if she had to, she would gladly do it all over again if that was what her mate needed from her.

But for now, she was going to get even with him for leaving her in a bed alone, and not letting her wake up in his arms like he always wanted to.

Celine slipped into another one of his shirts, snuck into the bathroom, and while he was distracted with his shower filled up a glass of cold water. Thick steam hid her well, and since it was the morning after his heat, his senses wouldn't be alerted by picking up her scent.

Standing on tiptoe she reached up and dumped the water on his head.

Cole hollered. She put the glass back on the counter and giggled. Cole pulled back the curtain, glanced around quickly until his eyes landed on her.

"That was for letting me wake up alone," she told him in a matter of fact voice. "Don't let it happen again."

"Oh you're going to pay for that!" Cole didn't bother with turning the water off or getting a towel. He stepped out of the shower and Celine ran out of the bathroom.

She ran down the hall to the stairs and was about halfway down before he reached them. She couldn't stop laughing all the way down and toward the kitchen, but her fun came to a halt when she saw Drake leaning back against the counter, drinking a cup of coffee.

"Drake!" she gasped, "What're you doing here?"

"When I get my hands on you..." Cole skidded to a stop behind her, water dripping from his naked body. "Drake!"

Celine lowered her head. Heat quickly came to her face, yet a grin tugged at the corners of her lips.

"What...um, what're you doing here?" Cole stuttered.

"This is my house." Drake said with a chuckle, hand over his mouth appearing like he might bust a gut any moment. "You might want to get something on," he nodded towards Cole. "Before Carrick comes down to fix breakfast. Not sure I like the idea of her seeing your ass buck naked."

Celine lost it and laughed. Cole smiled and turned around, showing his ass fully to Drake. When he was back up the stairs, Drake lost it and laughed.

"What did you do?" he asked, wiping tears from his eyes. "To have him chasing you down the stairs naked?"

"Poured cold water over his head while he was in the shower," she answered with what she hoped was an innocent voice.

Drake broke out in a fresh wave of laughter and tears. "You didn't?"

She just smiled at him.

"You better watch yourself, he'll get even."

She winked at him. "I hope so. I'm going to get dressed too. Be back in a flash."

* * * *

Drake shook his head and smiled. His cell started ringing and he pulled it out of his back pocket and frowned when he saw a blocked number. Blocked number wasn't good, since this was a new cell and only his family had the number. He pushed the green button, with his frown still in place, and then brought the phone up to his ear. He had a funny feeling in his stomach, like this call wasn't going to be a good one.

"Who the hell is this?"

A laugh came over the line. A laugh that had the power to send one hell of a chill down his spine, making him feel like a child again. It was a laugh that no matter how much time went by, Drake was always going to remember and fear just a little bit.

"I see your personality hasn't improved much. Pity. I thought we might be able to do some business together."

Josh Stan. Drake closed his eyes, pushing those childhood fears back along with the bile that threatened to make him ill. Anytime he saw a photo of the man, Drake felt sick to his stomach, now that he was hearing his voice, that illness came at him ten times stronger than any photo could ever have had on him.

"What the fuck do you want?" Drake growled.

"And no manners. Well I can definitely see where he gets that from."

"What the hell are you talking about?"

"I'm sure by now you know about the experiment your grandfather started," Josh stated. "After all, your little spy has stolen a lot of information and something else quite valuable."

"What spy?"

Again, Josh laughed at him and it pissed Drake off even more. "Come on, Drake! Using a girl to do your dirty work is a new one. I always thought you were the kind of guy who did things himself."

Cole came down the stairs pulling a shirt over his head. He was dressed in jeans, no shoes, and looking at Drake in a questioning manner. Drake mouthed whom he was talking to and both of Cole's eyebrows went up in surprise.

"I don't need anyone to help me deal with you," Drake snapped. "What do you want?"

"Well here's the deal then. I need money, you have it, and now you're going to give me some of it."

It was Drake's turn to laugh, "Are you out of your mind? Why the hell would I give you money for your sick games?"

"Because it will make sure that my guests have clothes and food. You do want them to live don't you?"

Drake's stomach dropped. "You're going to blackmail me into paying you to keep your pets comfortable?"

Josh made a tsking sound on the other end. "Blackmail is such a nasty word. I'm simply asking a blood relative to help with the cost is all. You think it over, and I'll be in touch."

The line went dead and Drake could only stand there, lowering the phone slowly

"Drake?" Cole came up to him. "What's going on?"

"Where's Celine?" Drake spoke through his teeth, anger coming off him in waves.

"Taking a quick shower," Cole answered. "What the hell is going on?"

"Have you heard from Chase?"

Cole shook his head. "No, why?"

"That friend of his, she hasn't stopped has she?" He turned to face Cole. "I know she hasn't, so don't bother lying to me and just tell me what she knows!"

Cole frowned, "I don't know. Chase took off yesterday to go find her. He sort of figured that she wasn't stopping and afraid she might get herself into some kind of trouble. What the hell is going on?"

Drake took another deep breath rubbed his jaw and looked down at the floor. He was wondering about that phone call. Josh Stan had said 'blood relative', and in his gut, he was scared to death at just what those words might mean.

His mind went back to that time he spent with his grandfather. Drake closed his eyes when the memory came of what he took from him. His hands started to shake.

"That motherfucker," Drake growled under his breath. "You bastard!" he yelled.

"Drake?" Cole was frowning at him. "What's wrong?"

"Their blood," Drake pulled his phone back out. He was going to call his father. "Son of a bitch, they are related to me!"

* * * *

Kane watched Josh closely. The bastard was smiling, pacing with his cell phone up against this mouth. He heard everything that Josh said and he wasn't stupid. He could read between the lines. Josh called someone to whom Kane and Sasha were related. He wondered who and how. Was it a brother, an Uncle, their father? The only thing Kane knew for sure was it was a mystery that Josh wasn't going to share with him.

"Do you think he's going to pay?" Jason asked Josh.

Josh was still smiling when he turned to Jason. "Oh if his little spy tells him what she found, he'll pay. They are very family oriented."

"Doesn't mean he'll pay."

Josh walked up to his cage and Kane did nothing to still the growl from slipping past his lips. He hated these men with a passion. He wanted to rip them both to pieces, with his bare hands, then stand over their bodies, watching as their life slipped away. Even the pain between his legs couldn't still the hatred.

Kane, don't please!

His eyes left Josh to look at his sister. Sasha was shaking from the cold again and he wanted nothing more than to warm her. She shouldn't be cold. Ever!

"I need a sample, Kane." Josh grinned. "Are you going to give it to me nicely?"

Kane moved his eyes from Sasha to Josh, back to Sasha before fixing his eyes on Josh and leaving them on him. "For blankets."

Josh laughed. "So the bastard is trying to negotiate. I'm almost impressed." He snapped his fingers and a guard pulled the collar attached to a chain around Kane's neck, yanking him back against the bars of the cage. The guard then opened the door and Josh stepped in. "You want blankets for her you're going to have to breed for them."

Josh stuck the needle in his neck. Kane growled loudly but couldn't stop them from pumping the drugs into his system. In an instant, he was weak and his vision blurry.

"The next time our guest shows up, Jason, please have her stay longer." Josh kept his eyes on Kane. They let Kane go and he dropped to the floor, but managed, somehow, to keep his eyes on Josh. "Kane wants to earn some blankets for his sister. Get the subject ready for him."

"Look what I've got!" Thad Palma, head of security walked in with two of his men dragging in a half conscious man. "Thought he might come in handy for your breeding experiments."

Kane shook the fogginess from his eyes to see what was going on. Josh looked from him to Sasha before he spoke. "Put him in a cage next to the girl." Josh walked up to Kane's cage with a nasty little grin on his lips. "Looks like I might have a use for your pretty sister after all."

Kane used the last bit of his energy to lunge at him. He snarled, "Touch her. I'll kill you."

"I do enjoy your enthusiasm, Kane." Josh smiled. "Quite enjoyable." He turned his back on Kane. "Get the new girl ready. If Kane gives us any trouble, toss Sasha into the cage with the male. I trust you won't give me any trouble?" Josh asked over his shoulder.

"One day Josh, your ass is mine," Kane growled low and deadly. "One day."

Chapter Nine

Jada paced the room, glancing over at Chase every few steps. His fever wasn't going down and the bullet hole in his leg, was bleeding like a bitch. She didn't have a clue what to do. When he had managed to walk over to use the bathroom, she heard him in there being sick too. It was definitely *not* good.

She wiped him down with wet cloths for a couple hours, but it did very little. With his help, she was able to strip him down to his boxers and get him into the tub for a cool shower. Chase shook and groaned about the cool water and she was shocked speechless when steam actually came off him.

"Chase, I need to call someone," she told him while she paced.

"N...No," he stuttered. "I...I'll be...fine."

"The hell you will be!" She rushed over to him on the bed, going down on her knees next to the bed. "You're sick and bleeding. We need help here. I can't get the fever down. You said so yourself that you were allergic to this shit. I'm pretty sure the bullet is still in your leg causing this crap and I can't take it out."

He didn't answer her, which helped with her making the decision. When Chase fell back asleep, Jada took his phone and slipped outside. The sun was shining brightly taking some of the crisp morning air away. It should have been one of those lazy days at home, reading a book or watching a show, but she was in a motel room watching one of her only friends bleed to death.

She flipped the phone open and started to go through the address book looking for a number. When she found the one she was looking for, she pressed the green call button, put it up to her ear, and waited. It rang and rang until the voice mail came on.

"Shit," she mumbled, closing the phone. "The one person I need and you're not fucking there. Damn you, Cole."

Jada paced in front of a few doors stopped and flipped the phone open again. She found another number and dialed it, not knowing what he was going to say once she told *him* what's up.

"Hi," she stopped pacing when someone answered. "Is this Drake?"

"Who's this?"

"Jada."

"Where's Chase?" He sounded angry on the phone. Had a slight growl to his voice when he spoke.

"I'm...I'm trying to get a hold of his brother, Cole. Do you know where I can reach him?"

She frowned when she heard mumbling on the other end.

"Jada!" Cole came on the line and she sighed with relief. "What the hell's going on? Where's Chase?"

"He's hurt," she answered. "Real bad."

"What?" he sighed loudly.

"We were followed. When we tried to get away, one of the men who'd been following us shot Chase," she went on quickly. "Two of the bullets went through him, one is still in his leg which is still bleeding, and he's burning up with a fever. You need to come."

"He got shot!" Now he was yelling.

Jada rubbed her forehead and tried to keep calm. "Yes," she said through her teeth. "And he needs your help."

"Where are you?"

"Highway one-ninety, exit twenty-nine B. Comfort Inn, the room all the way in the back. One thirteen. Knock four times so I'll know it's you." She hung up and took a deep breath, letting it out slowly. "Now do I stay and wait, or leave?"

* * * *

"First I'm going to kill him, then her." Cole handed Drake his phone back before he turned from the kitchen and headed back to his room for his shoes and to tell Celine what was going on.

"What's going on?" Drake asked, following him over to the stairs.

He didn't answer Drake, but rushed to his room. Celine was just finishing up getting dressed and jumped when Cole burst into the room. Her eyes were wide, watching his every move as he went around, tossing things onto the bed.

She frowned at him. "What's wrong?"

"Chase is hurt," he answered, grabbing a bag and putting the clothes he'd tossed on the bed into it. "I'm going to him. Jada called me."

"Oh God," she quickly turned and started to toss clothes onto his pile. "I'm going with you."

"Celine—"

She raised her hand, silencing him. "Don't even say it. I'm going with you and that's final. You're going to need an extra pair of hands."

He stared at her, but couldn't say a damn word, thanks to his cock. He couldn't control the damn thing, which started to rise at the most inconvenient times. No one should look that hot or ready for another round the morning after a full moon. But Celine did in her tight jeans and overdrive attitude. She was ready to kick ass right by his side and he loved her for it.

Last night he was hard on her, completely out of control and she seemed to love it. She took everything he had to give and even helped push him over the edge. But to look at her right now you couldn't tell it. She was full of fresh energy.

"Okay," he had to clear his throat to finish speaking, but he sure as hell couldn't move his eyes away from her breasts or stop his mouth from watering. "No point in arguing with you. But just so you know. I'm just this far from fucking the holy hell out of you." He showed her with a tiny pinch of his fingers how close he was. "And only the fact that I don't know what kind of shape Chase is in is preventing me from doing just that."

She smiled at him. "You're such a tease."

Cole's mouth dropped and he was speechless again when she turned her back on him and went over to another bag on the floor.

Out back, Drake was waiting for them next to the jeep. He handed Cole a first aid kit.

"Carrick is fixing up some food for the two of you to take," Drake said. "I called your dad and mine. They both want us back at the house. You find Chase and get him there. Call me as soon as you're heading there and I'll have the Doc waiting to look at Chase. There's a good chance he was shot with copper since he has a high fever and the bullet is still in him is causing all the problems. If you can, get it out and duct tape his ass to get him home.

Cole cocked his head to the side, handing the kit to Celine. "What else is on your mind?"

Drake rubbed his jaw. "My gut is telling me Josh Stan is about to strike again, but it's what he said that has me bugged." he turned toward Celine. "Take these," he handed her a set of brass knuckles.

"Ah, you give me the best presents," she smiled right before kissing him on the cheek.

"It's the family thing?" Cole stated.

Drake nodded. "If those two are our family, I need to know whose."

"But you already know, don't you?" Cole asked.

Drake slapped him on the shoulder. "Go take care of your brother and keep your phone on. I'll be in touch," he said instead of answering him.

Cole loaded the back of his Jeep with food that Carrick had put together. Before they left, Celine made a quick call to her father. Personally, he would feel a lot better if she was going with Drake back to the city. His gut was screaming that something wasn't right and Cole didn't want his mate to get hurt.

After they left, his mind was on his brother, and on his condition. What he was planning to say to Jada had him so worked up, he didn't say a word to Celine. He didn't know Jada that well. Didn't know if he could trust her, and wasn't sure about her loyalty towards his brother. Cole's gut instincts were telling him she not only knew more about what was going on, but she was more involved than any of them knew.

They reached their exit on the highway about an hour later, his mind still on Chase. If his brother was indeed shot with copper then anything left inside him for any length of time could kill him.

Shifters are very allergic to copper. If enough of it was in their system, it could turn their blood into poison. Even a graze on their body by anything having copper in it could cause a major infection. Cole had heard of a guy who was cut on the leg by a copper knife. The guy had lost his leg because of an infection his body couldn't fight. He just hoped like hell that didn't happen to Chase.

"He's going to be fine," Celine said, taking hold of his hand. "Just keep telling yourself that or you're going to drive yourself crazy."

He nodded and kept his eyes fixed on the road, "I have been, and I'm feeling very guilty."

"About?"

"I want to get to my brother, but I also want to pull over to the side and have my wicked way with you." He couldn't keep the growl from slipping out.

She giggled softly and put his hand on her leg, moving it up to her thigh to feel the heat between her legs. "Then how about this," she sighed. "When we get to the house, you can have your way with me in my old room. Always wanted you to seduce me in my bedroom."

"With pleasure," he purred, removing his hand from between her legs, only so he could concentrate on the road and not her sweet body.

They turned on highway one-ninety. Celine kept a watch out for the signs while he kept an eye out to see if they were being followed. The hairs on the back of his neck stood up in caution and he was listening.

"Here's the exit." Celine pointed out with her finger.

Cole nodded and took the turn. "Keep an eye open for the motel."

It took close to thirty minutes before they saw a sign that announced the motel. When they turned into the drive, Cole felt very uneasy. The place was dark and had an abandoned feeling to it.

They pulled around to the back and Celine pointed to a parked car. He pulled up to it and turned the Jeep off, but before he got out, he looked around to make sure they were alone.

"Do you have that funny feeling?" she asked.

"Yeah." He opened the door and slid out. Reaching for the bag Drake gave him he said, "I think as soon as I get his leg fixed we should move him."

He walked up to the door, glanced around, then knocked slowly four times. The wait killed him and he didn't even realize he was holding his breath until the door cracked open and sea green eyes stared out at him.

"Jada, open the door," he snapped.

Her eyes widened. She looked him up and down before the door slammed on his face. He thought she wasn't going to open up for him, which meant he was going to have to kick the door in but it didn't happen that way. He heard the chain slide and the door opened wide.

"Took you long enough." She nervously stepped back so Cole could enter.

Cole gave her a dirty look but his attention was quickly diverted to his brother, "Chase!" he rushed into the room and over to the bed where his brother lay.

Chase was out cold. His whole body was covered in sweat. He was in his boxers and the bandage around his right leg was soaked in blood, as was the one around his waist. When Cole touched Chase's forehead he shook his head. He was on fire.

"What happened?" he demanded, opening the bag up next to him on the floor.

"I was meeting Chase and someone followed me," Jada answered. "Chase was also followed. We got on his bike to leave, the rear tire was shot out and we crashed in a ditch. These guys came up, and I don't know. It all happened so fast. One second we were getting up to run away and the next he was being shot." She rubbed her face quickly. "I think I shot one, but I can't be sure."

"Celine, get me some towels and a bowl of cold water." He picked up his bag and walked around the bed so he could reach Chase's leg better. "How long ago?" When he didn't get an answer he glanced up and yelled at her, "How long ago?"

"Night after the full moon," Jada snapped back. "And before you try to rip me a new one I wanted to call you when it happened, but he wouldn't let me." She pointed at Chase.

Cole kept his eyes on her and pulled his knife out. Jada didn't even flinch once when he flicked his wrist and released the blade. They stared at each other until Celine came back in the room with the ice bucket full of water and all the towels and washcloths she could find in her hands.

Cole cut the wrapping from Chase's leg and inspected the wound. "The bullet's still in there."

"Yeah, I figured," Jada remarked with an emotionless voice.."

Cole inspected the leg closely. Each time he moved it a fresh blood came oozing out. "I'm going to have to dig it out." He took the water and a towel from Celine and put them on the floor next to him. He then brought out the syringe, filled it up with something from a glass bottle he brought out of his bag and stuck it in Chase's leg. "Okay, Celine, get on his chest and I mean sit on him with all your weight. You," he snapped his fingers at Jada. "Hold his leg down with all of your body weight. Sit on it, I don't care, just keep it down."

"Ever thought about saying please?" Jada grumbled under her breath.

Cole filled the syringe up again and held it at an angle right above the wound. "He's going to come unglued when I start to dig this out, so get ready."

He slid the needle in and shoved the contents of the syringe in at the same time. Chase didn't wake up or yell until Cole cut the wound wider and shoved his fingers into it, searching for the bullet. Cole had to change spots with Jada, sitting on Chase's leg as he dug around for it. His fingers burned, telling him that he had found it, just had to pull it out. Right before he pulled it out, Chase passed out and Cole was relieved he wouldn't be awake while he finished up. He filled up a larger syringe with a cleaning solution and put it right inside the wound, flushing all the copper out.

He washed the leg, sewed it up, and rewrapped it. Jada moved away and sat at the small table, one leg crossed over the other, watching. Cole kept his eyes on her when he stood up. He didn't see Celine, he assumed she was out getting Chase some clean clothes.

"There's more you're not telling me," he said.

"You're right." She crossed her arms over her chest and moved her ankle back and forth. "And I'm not *going* to tell you, either."

Cole chuckled, "You have balls, girl. I'll give you that." She glanced down at her watch and he frowned. "Got somewhere you need to be?"

"As a matter of fact, I do." She stood up.

"Tough," he pointed back down with his finger. "Sit down."

Celine came in with all three bags in her arms and once the door was open, Jada made her move.

"Hey!" Cole yelled when she grabbed her bag on the floor, and ran out the door, almost knocking Celine down. He chased her across the parking lot but lost her when she took a right into some trees. "Argh!" he yelled.

He walked back to the room and slammed the door closed.

"She ran." Chase was awake and sitting up in the bed. He had red circles under and around his eyes and specks inside. The look might have said hung over if you didn't know what had happened. The red around his eyes was from the copper. Some of it was in his blood stream and he needed medication ASAP to remove the poison.

"How do you feel?" Cole asked him, going back to his side quickly.

"Like shit," Chase sighed. "Can't believe she called you."

"If she hadn't—" he let the thought trail off. "What happened?"

"Maybe I should ask you that question." Chase glanced at Celine before he stared at him. "It appears that you two are getting along pretty well."

"We're just peachy." Celine smiled. "Unlike you it seems. You know I think you can give your brother a run for his money with the good looks and nice body."

Chase smiled and blushed. If she had said something like that to his brother a few days ago he might have gone into a dominating mode, but not now. He knew she was his for life.

"So how bad was it?" Chase asked.

Cole crossed his arms over his chest. He kept his face serious while he looked his brother in the eye. "You had a copper bullet in your leg. So that would rank right up there with pretty damn bad. I would like to get you the hell out of here, but your leg is still bleeding, so is your side. Plus you have a fever and I'm pretty sure a nice infection." He tapped a finger on his lips. "So I am going to go out on a limb here and say you are fucking sick and I need to get a doctor to look at your sorry ass."

"Give him a break," Celine sighed.

"Just as soon as he has healed." Cole smiled, but it was anything but a cheerful smile. "I'm going to kick your ass as soon as you are better, little brother. You promised me!" He pointed his finger at him, but before he could finish yelling at him Celine put herself right in front of him.

"Behave, or you don't get to play later," she whispered.

Chase chuckled, "I think she has you wrapped real tight." He coughed and that had them both facing him. "And it hasn't stopped bleeding," he sighed.

Cole rushed over to him and pulled the blankets back. Sure enough, the bed was soaked with blood. Chase was starting to look very pale and weak, which meant Cole needed to get him the hell out of here now before he bled to death.

"Shit," he mumbled.

"Think there's more in there?" Celine asked.

"I think it nicked something," Cole answered.

They jumped when someone banged on the door. Cole and Celine both looked at each other. No one knew where they were. Cole wondered if they were followed or if someone was still searching for Chase and Jada.

"Who is it?" Cole yelled.

"Police."

Cole mouthed fuck and covered his brother before standing up. Celine also followed him and pressed herself against the wall, behind the door, taking out the brass knuckles Drake had given her. He nodded to her and unlocked the door, leaving the chain on. The moment he opened it the door was kicked in and two guys forced their way inside.

Cole swung at the first guy, knocking him down, but he didn't go down easy. He took Cole with him and the two started to wrestle on the floor.

"Hey!" Celine yelled.

Cole looked up, fearing that the other one had his hands on Celine. That thought gave him the extra strength to overpower the one on top of him. Celine brought down one of the chairs over the back of the other, bringing him to his knees. Then she shocked Cole by kicking the guy in the face. The one on him had Cole pinned to the floor and a knife aimed at his chest—a brownish knife, which told him it was made out of copper.

Celine came up behind him and with her hands fisted together she hit him in the back. That brought his attention to her, but she acted fast. She hit the guy in the face with her brass fist, knocking him out.

Cole was lying there, breathing hard, "Where'd you learn that shit?"

"Hello, have you met my family?" She walked past him to Chase, and he rolled over to his feet.

"Had to be Drake," he mumbled.

"Partly, yes." She smiled at him. "Come on. Let's get Chase out of here. I don't know how long those two are going to stay out."

Celine took the bags and Cole picked Chase up. He was still bleeding, but they couldn't stay for him to try to fix it.

"Damn you're heavy," Cole said.

"Does that mean you're not going to carry me over the threshold?" Chase teased in a weak voice.

"Yeah, and don't ask me to kiss you." He put Chase in the back of his Jeep, then grabbed Celine by the arm, pulling her away so Chase wouldn't hear. "Call Drake. Something else is wrong and I think he needs the doctor."

She reached out and touched his face. "He's going to be fine."

Cole nodded, wrapped his hand around her wrist, and pressed his face in her hand for a second longer before pulling away and going back to check on Chase while she made the call.

"The shit you get yourself into." He shook his fist at Chase.

"I'll be fine," but Chase didn't sound fine, he sounded tired and too weak to talk. "We need to find Jada. She has something Cole. Something that could get her killed if they get their hands on her."

"What?" Cole never felt fear for a human before, but the way his brother talked about his friend, and the direction this whole private war has been going, anything was possible. If Chase was worried that the girl could get herself killed then it was something he was going to have to look into.

"I don't know. She wouldn't tell me, but I've got this feeling."

"Dad said the doc will be there by the time we get to the house," Celine butted in. "He's also sending you a short cut that should cut our driving time by at least an hour, depending on how fast you drive."

Cole nodded, his eyes on his brother. "When we get you fixed," he shook his finger at Chase, "The two of us are going to have one serious ass talk. This is twice you've added age to me with your stunts little brother."

Chase nodded also, but his eyes drifted shut once again.

"I don't know who I'm going to kill first," Cole sighed, rubbing his face and getting back into the Jeep. "Him or that girl."

"One thing at a time."

Cole floored it, spitting rock and dirt behind his wheels. Jada. Yep, that was the one he was going to put his hands around the throat of first. Because if it wasn't for her getting herself into trouble then his brother would be home sleeping in his new bed without a hole in his leg.

"Her." He stated, nodding. "When I get my hands on her I swear I'm going to choke her."

"Stand in line," Celine snorted. "I got a strong feeling Drake wants to also."

Chapter Ten

They pulled up to the Draeger house around five in the morning. Cole had to pull over a few times while Celine rewrapped Chase's leg. They were out of gauze and he was still bleeding, going in and out of consciousness, causing them both to worry. She wasn't a doctor, but she knew that Chase had lost a lot and was still losing blood. If he didn't get help fast then he might die.

Her family didn't waste time. Her father and the family doctor, Dr. Sager, waited for them with the front door open. Before Cole had the Jeep at a complete stop even, Dedrick and the doctor were getting Chase out of the back seat.

Cole quickly got out and rushed to help carry his brother inside. Celine hung back to get everything out of the Jeep. She was very tired and didn't want to be in the way. She was surprised when her Uncle Adrian snuck up behind her.

"How's it going, kid?" Adrian took the bags from her and wrapped one arm around her shoulder. She was so tired that all she could do was grin and lean against him, as they walked toward the house. "That bad, huh?"

"I'm very tired," she sighed.

"I bet. Day after full moon is supposed to be a day to rest, not save the world." She chuckled. "Come on. Your mom left some food in the fridge, so let's get it warmed up for everyone."

Shifters 5: Cole's Awakening

Adrian dropped the bags next to the front door and pulled Celine to the left toward the kitchen in the back. Adrian pushed her down into a chair. Celine went very willingly.

Five kids and her Uncle still looked like a man in his mid-thirties. Not one speck of gray touched his sandy blonde hair, and not one ounce of flab touched his body.

"So where are my mother and two aunts?" she asked.

Adrian pulled out a large pan of cold chicken and set it on the counter before turning to face her. "Your dad had your mother and Aunt Sidney head up to Heather's. Skyler went with the kids. Thought it might be best to try and keep everyone safe, until we know for sure what is going on."

"Am I supposed to join up with them also?"

Adrian shrugged, "Don't know. Hungry?"

She shook her head and stood up. "I think I'm going to clean up and try to get Cole to take a nap. He drove straight here and hasn't had much sleep."

"That might be a good idea. He could get in the good old Doc's way if she has to cut into that leg."

Celine nodded and left the kitchen. She picked up the bags from in front of the door and headed upstairs.

Chase had been taken to one of the guest rooms instead of her bedroom. The door was left cracked open and she was able to see some of what was going on.

Chase laid on the bed, the doctor hovering over his leg. He was out cold and her father handed things to the doctor when she asked for it. Apparently, the woman was doing surgery on the leg. She didn't see Cole, but did jump when an arm wrapped around her waist.

"They're working on his leg," Cole whispered in her ear. "The bullet nicked an artery, which is why he never stopped bleeding."

"Is there any copper left?"

"No," he sighed and rested his chin on top of her head. "But there is some poison from it in his blood. She gave him a shot to help fight the infection and flush it out of his system. She thinks we saved his life. If the bullet stayed in there much longer then the infection would have been too much to fight and he would've died."

She turned around in his arms and hugged him tight before stepping away and taking hold of his hand, pulling him behind her. "Come on. You need some rest."

He didn't fight her. She led him to her room, closed the door behind them and pushed him so he was sitting down on the bed. Celine helped him take his shoes and shirt off, and then Cole stood up and let his jeans drop to the floor. She tucked him in the bed. He was asleep before she was undressed and under the covers next to him.

Morning came too soon for her. They woke together, showered together, but didn't make love as she sort of hoped for. Cole went to check on Chase and she headed down stairs to fix a late breakfast. Celine was surprised to find her father and Uncle Adrian sitting at the kitchen table drinking coffee.

"You two are up early," she stated, heading right for the fridge for some juice.

"Never went to sleep." Adrian smiled.

"How's Chase?" she asked her dad.

"Patched up." Dedrick sighed. "He's going to be laid up for a few weeks. His leg was in pretty bad shape and he lost a lot of blood. She set up a transfusion for him and will be back in a few hours to give him another."

"Have you heard from Drake yet?" She sat down and grabbed a muffin from the plate in the middle of the table.

"Yeah, said he was trying to find Jada but couldn't, so he's heading here and should show up in a couple of hours," Dedrick answered.

"He isn't going to find her," she stated. "I'm pretty sure she's very good at hiding out and staying hidden."

"Can't hide forever," Adrian snickered. "We'll find her."

"Dad, I'm worried about her," Celine said. "If she has come across something important, wouldn't these people kill to keep it hidden?"

"First, it depends on what she has found, but I'm going to say yes," Dedrick nodded. "Josh Stan is the kind of guy who would kill to keep his secrets."

"What do you think she could have taken then?"

"I would say proof of his experiments," Adrian butted in. "That man has a lot to keep hidden."

"I don't understand how someone could create one of us to keep in a cage and torture all of his life." She shook her head and sighed. "So cruel."

"Well, old man Martin wasn't one for having a very sane mind," Dedrick groaned, standing up and going over to the coffee pot. He filled his cup. "He thought there was a cure for what we are and until the day he died, he tried to find it."

"Don't forget about trying to eliminate us, too," Adrian added.

Cole walked in and she quickly stood up. "Want something to eat?"

"Only if you're cooking it." Cole smiled, kissed her on the cheek, and then sat down in the seat she had vacated.

Celine went over to the fridge and pulled out some eggs and sausages. "Dad, Uncle Adrian, you two want anything?"

"Honey, I'll never turn food down." Adrian smiled.

She made a large bowl of scrambled eggs and fried the sausages. The four of them ate, and Adrian helped clean up the mess. Cole told them how Chase was resting, the medication Doctor Sager gave him was still in effect. He figured that Chase might wake up sometime in the afternoon, and Celine was already planning on what he was going to eat. Shifters ate a lot, and when they were sick, they could eat even more.

About an hour, later Drake and Brock came in. Drake looked mean and depressed. A clear sign that something was wrong.

"We need to have a family meeting," Drake growled. "Right now!" He stormed out of the kitchen and the rest of the family followed him.

* * * *

"Want to tell me that again?" Drake paced the living room pissed off. He knew that Cole had lost Jada, again, and it still pissed him off. "Just so I didn't misunderstand."

"You heard me," Cole said, leaning against the wall while Drake paced.

"She ran on you." Drake stopped pacing, ran a hand in his hair and growled. "She fucking *ran* and you didn't catch her!" he yelled. "How the hell did that happen?"

"No point in getting upset," Dedrick said calmly. "Anger isn't going to find her."

"No, but me choking the shit out of her will help me!" Drake snapped. "So where did she go?" He shoved his hands into his jean pockets because if he didn't, he might just put his hands around Cole's throat.

"I don't know," Cole sighed.

"Great!" He picked up a lamp and threw it as hard as he could against the wall. He was so pissed off he saw red.

"When is your dad supposed to show up?" Dedrick asked, his voice calm.

"I'm here," Stefan walked in alone. He was the one who'd gone to take the girls over to Heather and Brock's place after Brock left to join up with Drake. "You're going to pay for that?" He pointed at the crushed lamp.

"I thought Carrick tamed that damn temper of yours." Brock grinned before he slumped down on the sofa, linked his fingers together over his chest, and looked up at Drake. "So give. Why the sudden male only meeting? And why is Celine here?"

"It's about Kane and Sasha." Drake took a deep breath, one hand went to the back of his neck and rubbed. "Jada sent Chase the information on their parentage and I have it. *And* I don't think she wanted me to know about it either." He gave Celine a quick glance. "And Cole's letting her stay for our meeting."

"So who is it?" Brock asked.

Drake took a deep breath and let it out in a rush. "The mother was a human that Martin experimented on. It is reported that she died when he extracted eggs from her. Bled to death. Five he tried to fertilize, only one took and grew in a test tube until he was able to find a surrogate to carry the child to full term."

"Sick bastard," Stefan mumbled.

"The egg split," Drake went on. "They froze one. Grew it in a test tube for a few months before finding another woman to implant the egg into. The girl wasn't grown until the boy was about eight, I think. They thought she would help keep him under control."

"What, they are twins eight years apart?" Dedrick asked. "That's strange."

"Wait, you said that Josh told you they were family," Brock remarked in a rush, his hand up.

"They are." Drake couldn't look at them all. Each set of eyes that were on him was an extra reminder of what happened years ago. He turned his back to them and tried to get the bile that was rising back down. Just knowing what he knew made him sick. Knowing what they were doing to his blood made him want to kill, and that was very dangerous.

"Drake?" Stefan said.

Drake swallowed hard but still didn't turn around to them. "*I'm* their father."

The silence in the room added to the weight in his shoulders and he hung his head. Drake always knew. Deep down he *knew* that a part of him had been taken and left behind. He felt pain that didn't belong to him or his brother, pain that he could never explain. Now it all made sense.

"You want to say that again?" Stefan asked. "Because if I heard you right, which I'm thinking I didn't, you said you were their father."

Drake steeled himself for the worst and turned back around to face his family. "That's what I said."

Stefan shook his head, "No. That isn't possible!"

"We didn't get it all," Dedrick mumbled to Stefan.

"Does someone want to tell me what's going on?" Brock asked, standing back up.

"Bullshit!" Stefan yelled at Dedrick. "We took everything."

Brock whistled loudly, getting everyone's attention. "What the hell is going on?"

Drake looked from his father to his Uncle. Stefan and Dedrick were having a stare off. The tension continued to mount

"Dear old granddad, damn him, took something from me when I was caged up," Drake answered his brother. "Young sperm so he could make his own breed for testing. I've got a son who is almost my own age as well as a daughter who is eight years younger than her brother."

* * * *

"Wow." That was all Cole could say after the meeting was over. He filled Chase in on what happened, glad that his brother was finally awake. "Of all the things I could have thought possible, that wasn't one of them."

Cole was a little surprised to find Chase trying to get up and use the bathroom. Cole dashed into the room just before his brother fell flat on his face, catching him. He picked Chase up and put him back in bed, then handed him a bedpan which had been left in the room for bathroom breaks. Chase bitched about having to pee like this, but Cole bitched right back about what kind of shape his leg was in and that he almost bled to death. For at least a week, he was pissing in a cup if he had to.

Thanks to his little stunt, his leg bled lightly, but nothing the doctor needed to come back for. Celine brought him some broth to drink, changed the bandage on his leg and sat at the foot of the bed until he was finished, listening to them.

"And she didn't tell me," Chase sighed. "Unbelievable."

"How well do you know her?" Celine asked.

Chase scratched his head then rubbed his face before answering. "Jada was the quiet one. Met her at college. She was taking pictures, think photography was her major or something, and she kept to herself. If memory serves me right, I think a grandfather sent her to a boarding school, but never knew why." He looked at Cole. "She's damn good at getting information. Like hacker good and has an eye like you don't see very often. I've seen some of the photos she takes, which is what she used to do for money and they are damn good. Gallery good if you ask me."

"When did she find out about you?" Cole asked, sitting down next to Celine, draping an arm over her shoulders.

"Couple months after we started hanging out together," Chase sighed. "Freaked me the hell out too. Thought she was going to tell everyone, but she was cool about it. Said I was her only friend and she didn't want to mess it up. No one in school had anything to do with her."

"Why?" Celine frowned.

"They thought she was strange," Chase chuckled. "But she just says what's on her mind. Doesn't hold anything back, if you know what I mean?"

Celine smiled, "Tells it like it is, huh? I could like that."

Chase nodded, "Yep. She's kept my secret for years, Cole. I trust her."

"But how smart is she when it comes to staying out of trouble?" Cole crossed his arms over his chest.

"Not very." Chase winced when he moved in the bed.

Celine pointed at him, "You bust those stitches I'm going to kick your ass."

Cole smiled. "Don't test it. Believe me, I've seen her in action. Has a mean right hook."

"You're worried about her." It was a statement not a question and Chase met Cole's eyes.

Cole nodded.

"You think she went back there," Chase went on. "Why?"

"That's what I'm hoping you can tell me." Cole took a deep breath. "Why would she go back there?"

Chase shrugged. "As far as I know she has all the information she needs. There's no reason for her to go back there. Only thing left that I know of is us getting a plan together and going in there before they move them again."

"Maybe that's it," Celine remarked, drawing their attention. "If he moves them, thinking that we know where they're at, then maybe she went back in order to keep an eye on them. Get the location."

"She has a point." Cole stood back up and started to pace. He stopped and pointed at the two of them. "You stay with him. I'll be right back."

He left the room and went downstairs to the office where Stefan, Dedrick, Brock, and Drake were talking. Without knocking, he walked in and they all stopped what they were doing to look up at him. Adrian was working on a computer.

"She's spying on them."

Drake frowned. "Who?"

"Jada," Cole answered. "She's back at that lab, spying on them more than likely to tell us where they go when they move."

"You think they're going to move the lab again?" Stefan asked.

"Yes," Drake answered, keeping his eyes on Cole. "Josh knows someone is watching him and thinks we have planted a spy. He's looking for someone too."

Cole nodded, "And if she gets caught…"

"She's fucked," Drake finished.

"We need to find that lab," Dedrick said.

"And get them out," Drake whispered.

Stefan came up to Drake and put his arm around his shoulders. "It isn't your fault. We didn't know or even think it was possible that the man would do something like this."

"But it is," Drake sighed. "I felt like something wasn't right for so long and now I know why. I was feeling their pain."

"We need those files," Dedrick added. "We need to know everything about the two of them and what has been done." He rubbed his face, hands on his hips facing Drake. "If Kane has been tortured all his life then you can pretty much bet he's more animal than man. Don't look at him as your son, but a beast needing to be trained. He has to be taught how to function and learn all there is to know about being a shifter."

Drake nodded, "Best place for him to learn how to live like a free man is up in the woods. It's open, he can roam, have a place all his own."

Celine ran into the room with Chase's phone in her hand. "Jada," she panted. "Sent directions. Said they won't move them for a couple of days." She swallowed, licked her lips and appeared like she was trying to catch her breath. "Just beat the hell out of Kane."

"Fuck," Drake sighed, turning away from them all.

Cole looked from Stefan to Dedrick and waited. The brothers glanced at each other before Stefan finally spoke: "Okay then, we have twenty-four hours to hatch a plan and get them out."

"Is that going to be enough time?" Celine asked.

"We don't have a choice, CeeCee," Drake answered her. "Once Kane is healed enough to move, Stan is going to hide them again. As much as I hate to admit it, Jada has given us a small window here. We need to jump on it while it's cracked open."

"I understand that, but don't you think that he might suspect you will try and go in there to rescue them?" she added.

"She has a point, Drake," Stefan said. "Stan isn't stupid. He'll know that you would try to go in there and take them, especially when you find out that you're the father."

"Then what the hell do you suggest I do?" Drake asked through his teeth.

Stefan handed him his cell phone, "Call him."

* * * *

Josh Stan sat behind his desk in his leather chair looking at Sasha who was shaking, hands twisting together, her head lowered. Timid and useless. That was what this girl was, at least to some point. The only thing she was good for it seemed was to keep Kane in line, and that was starting to fail. He needed more leverage.

"Show it to me," he ordered.

Only one woman he trusted to keep a very thorough eye on the girl, and when she took her down for her monthly inspection, something caught the woman's eye. A birthmark that he'd never seen since he had taken things over. In fact, the mark wasn't even in Martin's notes. That meant it only started to form now that she was filling out and maturing.

Sasha was forced to turn around by the woman, her hair pulled over her left shoulder and the gown she was wearing ripped down her back to expose her right shoulder. She jumped some from the harsh treatment, but not much.

Josh sat forward. On the back of her right shoulder was a birthmark unlike anything he'd ever seen in his life. An open, dark black crescent moon. If it was just a bit further up on her shoulder it would look like a bite mark. The same kind of mark that those animals left on their mates.

"Has anyone else seen her mark?" he asked, slowly coming to his feet and walking around the desk. He moved closer and reached out, touching it.

"No sir," the woman answered.

He touched the mark, gliding his fingers over the dark curves. She shivered and curled her shoulders and head as if she was trying to curl herself up in a ball away from his touch.

"Maybe you have a use after all, girl," he murmured. "One that we don't know about."

He grabbed her arm roughly, yanking her from his office back down to the lab. She held onto her ripped gown as best as she could but instead of taking her back to her own cage, Josh went to their newest guest. He snapped his fingers, the guard unlocked the door and Josh shoved the girl inside, into the young man's arms.

"It's time I think to test if she can breed or not," he said. Kane growled loud, banging on the bars. Josh glanced over at Kane and then frowned when his cell went off, mostly because the few who had this number were here in the lab. "Who is this?" he demanded when he answered.

"Now look whose personality needs adjustment," Drake laughed. "I guess you have a thing about manners also."

Josh's eyes narrowed. "How did you get this number?"

"Stan, you're not the only one who can get things like phone numbers. I'm very resourceful when I need to be."

Josh snickered, "Well, I will assume then, this call is about the investment and you've changed your mind."

"Never assume anything. It only makes an ass out of you."

Josh saw red. He was used to being respected, so to be called an ass just pissed him off. "Be careful, Drake. Your actions could bring punishment to others."

"Oh I know, Josh. All of your dirty little secrets. I know it all. So does your daughter." His voice lowered, sounding almost threatening. "Do you get a rush knowing that you tortured not just one, but two kids? First me, and now my son."

That damn spy he had! His anger boiled over, but Josh kept it all under control. He strolled away from Sasha back to Kane. He stared down at Kane, tightly secured by his chains. Jason was going to beat Kane again, but he stopped the man. He didn't want him to bleed, but didn't stop him from taking Kane back to the chair. Another pounding would help keep the animal in line and down. But the disrespect in Drake's voice made Josh want Jason to draw blood. He wanted Kane to suffer since he couldn't have Drake. The son of a bitch who had taken his daughter from him.

"Call it even," Josh sighed. "You have my child, I have yours. Or children I might add, but the girl is useless. In fact, I was just checking her over myself, wondering if her use was gone. Don't like to keep dead weight you know."

Drake growled and Josh smiled. It gave him pleasure to torment the one who caused him pain. Drake Draeger was the only man who did that, only because he had Carrick.

"You know I could be inclined to make a sale," Josh sighed. "You can have the girl for a price."

"How about for your life?" Drake spoke low and slow. "I let you live and you give me both of them."

Josh laughed into the phone, "Oh, you are priceless. Your grandfather was wrong. You are definitely more than an animal. But I'm afraid I can't do that." He quickly sobered. "They are a very valuable asset. One that I don't intend to let go of any time soon. But I am thinking about creating another, in case Kane becomes useless. Would you like for it to be bred from a female of your kind, or another human?"

The phone went dead. Josh smiled big and put his phone back in his pocket, turned and headed back to his office. Kane was being dragged off for a fresh beating. He worried just a little because he wanted to create a drug to sterilize the bastards, not do it by beating his balls to tiny marbles.

"I'm going to set up the new lab," he said to Jason, coming to a stop in front of Kane's cage. "We're going to have to move soon. I have a strong feeling they are going to try and rescue my little experiments."

"I don't think they're that stupid," Jason snorted.

"Never underestimate your enemy." Josh held a finger up. "Drake wants them, and a desperate man will do anything to get what he wants." He cast a quick look over his shoulder at Sasha who was white as a sheet. "She has a mark that I want to look at closer. Once we get to our new home, we'll have to start testing on her. But make sure that he breeds on her. I want to know if she can or not after all."

* * * *

Cole jumped when Drake threw the phone at the wall, shattering it. He'd never seen Drake this angry before, and was very glad that anger wasn't directed at him when the knowledge that Celine was his mate came out. Drake could have torn him apart without blinking.

"We go tonight," Drake told them all, before storming out of the room.

"I'm going to take it the conversation didn't go well," Adrian remarked when Drake was gone.

"We don't have the shit to go in there tonight," Brock stated. "All we have is an address."

Stefan opened his mouth, but Adrian cut him off. "Don't get your knickers in a bind, Nancy. Got a load of shit in my trunk." He slapped his arm around Brock's shoulder, tugging him out of Dedrick's office. "Come on boy, let's go get our toys."

Cole frowned and moved his finger back and forth between the two, "Are they always like that?"

"Like what?" Celine asked.

"Well, they act like they're going to blow shit up or something."

"Oh that." Celine crossed her arms over her chest and glanced at where her uncle and cousin had been standing. "Oh yeah," she nodded. "I think Uncle Adrian was the instigator when it came to getting those two in trouble."

"Who the hell do you think showed them how to hack shit and blow crap up," Stefan shook his head. "And they turned around and showed

Celine."

Cole turned his frown toward Celine and she batted her eyes at him, trying to look innocent. "Guess there are a *few* things I still need to know about my mate."

Adrian and Brock came back inside. Both had large crates in their arms loaded with stuff that Cole really didn't want to know about.

"Think you can hold Drake off long enough so I can make a few of these?" Adrian asked Stefan.

"If he knows you are going to blow something up for him, I'm sure he'll give you a few hours," Stefan answered. "Just don't tell my wife, or my sister. They'll have both of our nuts."

Cole chuckled at Stefan when he walked past him to leave.

"Come on," Celine took his hand and tugged him out of the room. "You really don't want to be here for this."

"Sure you don't want to help, CeeCee?" Brock asked. "We can make an extra loud one for you." He shook some pipe and wires around like he was trying to entice her.

Cole wrapped his arm around her waist and picked her up when she acted like she was going to ditch him and play with Brock. She laughed as he carried her out, and he didn't put her down until they were half way up the stairs.

* * * *

Kane paced his cage, taking deep breaths, smelling something that was very different in the lab. Something that didn't belong. He tried to act normal and not direct the attention of his guards or the staff, but he couldn't sit down. Couldn't act like nothing was wrong when he could smell someone that shouldn't be here. Someone sweet. He also couldn't stop watching the man that Sasha was locked up with. So far, the guy hadn't touch her, which was good for him.

Kane closed his eyes and took a deep breath. He knew that scent. It was a female and she was hiding. The same female he had caught the scent of several times before.

He tried to look for her, without it being obvious. But it was hard. He felt so on edge at the moment and didn't trust the guy with his sister.

"And the animal stirs." Jason strolled in front of the cage with a smirk on his face. Kane growled. "You know we really don't give a shit if you talk or not, and the growling doesn't affect us at all."

The scent stirred and he fought to not look up. He struggled to keep his eyes on Jason.

"What has the mutt acting like this?" Jason went on, getting closer to the cage. "Is it the fact that your sweet little sister is going to be getting fucked soon?"

When he got close enough, Kane pounced on him. He grabbed a hold of Jason fast, wrapping his arm around his neck so tight that he cut his air off.

Kane growled again, low in Jason's ear. "I'm looking forward to the day I rip your fucking throat out with my bare hands."

Staff and guards rushed up to the cage and pried his arm from Jason's throat. Kane backed up, breathing hard and glared at them all. One day. One day he was going to get out of this cage and he was going to kill them all.

Jason rubbed his throat, "String him up." He took the dart gun from one of the men and aimed it at Kane. "Fuck you, dog," he shot and smiled when Kane dropped to his knees.

All of his strength left, leaving him helpless to fight back when they opened the door and cuffed him with the thick metal that would hold him up when his legs couldn't do it anymore. Jason was going to beat him and there wasn't a damn thing he could do about it when he was drugged. What sucked even more was that he hadn't completely healed from the last beating he took.

"Time to bleed, Kane."

Chapter Eleven

She could *not* watch them beat that guy, just for protecting his sister. There was no way without her giving her hiding place away and being caught. Because for Jada to keep her mouth shut while he was whipped was something she would never be able to do. So she moved and went into the office with the sole purpose of finding the leverage she needed to shut him down. She needed to find out where they were moving and give the information to Drake. After all, it was past time he knew about his kids.

Jada snooped around the dark office. She looked through papers, drawers, and filing cabinets until she found half of what she was looking for. An address for another warehouse which was already being set up just waiting for their guests. She cringed at the memory of the beating that was going on downstairs and couldn't get over how someone could do that to another person.

She stuffed the paper into her pocket but stilled when she heard a gun cock behind her and felt the barrel press against her head.

"So, you are our little snoop."

Jada grabbed the back of the desk chair with both hands. She didn't hesitate for even a second. She picked it up, swung as hard as she could to her right and hit the guard with all her might, smashing it over his head. He dropped to the ground.

"And you are out cold, asshole." She dropped the pieces of the chair in her hand, slung her bag over her shoulder and climbed back up into the old beams of the roof.

She crawled back into the ventilation system and headed back the same way she came in. She heard the yelling. The orders to find her and bring her back. But her plan was to get as far away from this place as possible.

At the end of the tunnel, she kicked the grate open, grabbed the top, and slid her way out. The moment her feet touched the ground she ran and didn't look back to see if anyone followed. She didn't have to. She knew she was being followed, and that left her with only one choice.

She ran until her side started to hurt and burn, but didn't stop. Jada ran to a closed gas station where she knew a working pay phone was located. It was about a half a mile from the building and she was pretty sure she could make it. All she had to do was push the pain in her side away.

When she saw it, she almost stopped running, she was that happy to see it. But time wasn't with her. She needed help, needed it now, and didn't have too many to call. And why the hell the disappointing thought of her lack of friends came to her at that moment, she didn't know. She didn't need to think of the friends she *didn't* have but needed to focus on the one she did have, because right now he was the only one who could help her. Sad part, Jada didn't even know if she could call him a friend or not.

She quickly put some change in and dialed the number that Chase gave her in case of extreme emergencies, and right now, she was having one of those. While it rang, she looked around to make sure she was still alone. So far so good.

"Hi, is this Drake or Brock?" she demanded the second the other end was answered.

"Drake. Jada?"

"Yeah, dumb ass Jada here. Listen they caught me and I'm pretty sure they are following me," she stuttered out fast, gulping air into her lungs.

A twig snapped, and Jada thought her heart was going to stop. She moved the phone from her ear and turned around to look. Jada screamed when a hand busted through the glass. She dropped to the floor, grabbed some of the glass, and cut the hand that was trying to cover her mouth with a cloth. The guy yelled and she ran out, leaving the phone hanging.

* * * *

"Jada!" Drake yelled into the phone. "Jada! Answer me!" Hearing nothing, he growled and threw his second phone for the night on the dashboard of the hummer, "Fuck."

"What happened?" Cole sat forward in his seat.

"They got her," Drake answered, his anger going straight to boiling point. Now for sure he was going to take matters into his own hands when it came to that girl. "Jada went back to that fucking lab, and got caught," he said through his teeth.

"Aw shit," Cole sighed, sitting back and rubbing his face.

"They're after her now," Drake went on. "And I'm pretty damn sure they got a hold of her too."

"How far away are we from the warehouse?" Cole asked Brock.

"Ten minutes at the most," Brock answered. "Calm down, Drake."

Drake held up his hand with an automatic gun and slid the chamber before turning to his brother. He was calm, but not the kind of calm he was sure his brother wanted to see. "Oh I'm calm brother. You have *nooooo* idea, how fucking calm I am."

"Not good," Brock glanced at Cole in the rearview mirror.

"Drake—" Cole started to say.

"The next one of you who tells me to calm down, I'm going to pound the fuck out of him," Drake snarled. "That motherfucker has taken enough from us! My Goddamn cells so he can make his own breed, then beats him. I swear to Christ if Kane can't walk out of that building I'm going to burn it all down."

"Well at least we are at an understanding," Brock sighed with a grin. "Hate to go in there without a plan."

"I'd floor it if I were you," Cole said softly to Brock. "Drake is in a hurry to do some major destruction."

Brock nodded, "Point taken."

* * * *

Jada fell to the ground hard and rolled over, got back to her feet and took off at a run. She skidded to a halt when a large truck with bright spotlights hit her in the face, blinding her. She heard the distinctive sound of many guns being cocked while she stood there breathing hard.

Gasping for breath, Jada raised her hands above her head in surrender. Several times, she licked her lips and looked around, trying to find some way of escaping this. Someone shoved the barrel of a gun into her back and she hissed.

"Do you mind? Stop shoving that thing in my back." she said. "It's a bit uncomfortable."

"Move!" one of the men ordered, shoving her from behind.

"What, no please?" Another sharp jab and she was walking towards the truck.

Hands still up in the air she was roughly yanked into the truck and pushed down to the floor. Once the door closed, she turned to one of the men who had a gun pointed at her face.

"You sure do go to a lot of trouble for just one girl." She smiled. "What do you do when a girl says no after you asked her out on a date?"

The man took his foot and shoved her back down to the floor face first, "Shut the fuck up." he snapped.

"Don't take rejection well," she mumbled to herself. "I will keep that in mind."

The moment the truck pulled to an abrupt stop, Jada knew she was back at the lab. She closed her eyes and groaned when the man who'd leaned on her back took her arm roughly and yanked her out of the truck.

This time she walked through front door into the lab. She looked around at everything while she walked. Things sure did look different when you were going in from the front door instead of looking down through the ventilation ducts.

"So this is our little spy?"

Jada looked at the tall man with cruel eyes and an even meaner smile. A chill went down her spine at the bold way he looked her up and down.

"You bitch!" The guard that she hit with the chair pushed his way toward her and slapped her so hard she fell down. She tasted blood on her lip and swore under her breath at the burn from a cut lip.

She slowly stood back up and narrowed her eyes on him. "Oh, I hit you with the chair, right?" He nodded with eyes slit and his lip curled up.

"Then this shouldn't come as a surprise." She kicked him hard between his legs, bringing him down to his knees. "Don't choke on your marbles."

The one who acted like he was in charge chuckled. "You sure do have balls." He licked his lips. "Such a pretty thing, too. I bet you taste as good as you look."

He reached out to touch her face but she jerked away from him. "I bet you're Jason." She pointed at him before tapping her lip thoughtfully. "The prick." She snapped her fingers and smiled.

He laughed again. "I'm going to enjoy breaking you."

"Eat your Wheaties," she said and smiled.

"She made a call," one of the other guards said.

"Is that so?" Again those cold eyes roamed over her body. "Who did you call?" he asked with a smile that didn't reach his eyes.

Jada crossed her arms over her chest, leaned to the left on one foot and cocked her head to one side. She glared up at him, "None of your damn business," she informed him with her chin up.

He laughed, and then out of nowhere, he backhanded her. That was twice now that she'd been slapped and she promised herself there wasn't going to be a third. In fact, she charged him but rough hands held her back. Even though she only stood at five-two, and had a small frame, it never stopped her from standing up for herself or for others who were being abused.

"Jason!"

Jada turned at the sound of a faint, yet very pissed off voice. She reached up to her burning cheek, rubbing the pain away and her eyes bugged out at what they found. The one who she had taken photos of, Kane, was chained to a wall, his back toward them, bloody. They were fresh, and she couldn't suppress the groan that slipped past her lips. His back was raw and it had her hurting for him. Lowering her eyes, she saw fresh bruising on his lower body, which made her cringe. Not only had he been whipped, but it looked like something beat the holy hell out of his nuts. Now that had to be beyond painful.

"Well, look who has decided to wake up and join our party," Jason said. "Have something to say?" he asked in a sweet voice.

"I'm going to kill you!" Kane yelled.

"Can't say as I blame him," she whispered back with a smile. "You're kind of a prick."

Jason grinned at Jada once more before he backhanded her again. This time when she swayed to the side, she grabbed a knife from one of the men standing next to her and swung it wide. She stabbed Jason deep into his arm.

Jason screamed and Kane howled. Kane's eyes locked with hers when he turned his head, causing Jada to stop before she made a move. Never in her entire life had she seen a man who looked this powerful. His eyes alone told the tale of how hard he had it. When she saw the redness of his eyes, she took a step back.

"You fucking bitch!" Jason yelled, pulling the knife from his arm and letting it drop to the floor. All attention was on Jada and what she had done so no one noticed what Kane was doing. But she did.

Kane stood his full six foot eight and snarled at Jason with his head turned. He showed everyone his canines as he began to change his form. His height changed and fur and more muscle mass took place all over his body. Jada watched with an open mouth. She had never seen Chase during his actual transformation, she'd only been told about it, and nothing she had been told matched what she was seeing right now.

His nose turned into a dog's snout. Hands and feet turned into paws with five fingers and toes with extremely sharp and long nails. Fur covered his whole body and since he didn't have clothes on, nothing ripped when he kept growing. Blood still coated his body, only it was fur and not flesh, and some of the striped wounds on his back healed with his change, but not the deep ones.

"I may be a bitch, but you're fucking dead!" she yelled back with a slight chuckle, snapping out of her fascination of the changed animal cuffed to the wall, or better yet, make that the one who was breaking his cuffs.

Jason turned to Jada and was about to hit her with a closed fist but stopped when the collar around Kane's throat broke off. It was the last restraint to hold him in place. Kane was free!

"Son of a bitch!" Jason yelled before he pushed Jada out of the way. "Someone get me a fucking gun!" he finished.

Jada fell to the ground and stared opened mouthed at Kane. He turned his wolf size head toward Jason and snarled. A guard came up to him but whatever the man was thinking about doing he didn't get to do it. One huge ass wolf hand came out and swung at the man, instantly breaking his neck.

"Damn," Jada gasped softly.

She watched while Jason managed to get his hands on a tranquilizer gun. He took aim and shot Kane about four times before Kane showed any signs of weakening. "You will go down you bastard!" Jason yelled.

Jason shot him three more times before Kane dropped down to his knees a few feet away from her. She scooted away from him when he reached out toward her. Her back touched a table leg at the same time an explosion hit the front door. The power of the doors bursting open and the wind that followed knocked Kane back away from her and Jada in another direction. When she glanced around to see where Jason might have gone, she spotted him running in the opposite direction of the front doors. Like the coward she knew him to be, just a kitty with his tail tucked between his legs!

"Figures," she mumbled.

"Knock, knock," a large man with dark hair and cold eyes walked inside, looking around. His blue eyes gave Jada the chills. She knew she did not want to mess with him.

"Anyone home?" another one came inside and he looked just like the first. Standing together Jada knew that she was staring at the Draeger twins. And they were one hell of a formidable image.

In what felt like slow motion, Jada watched Cole walk in behind the two. Shots went off everywhere and men tried to run and duck out of the way. She covered her head just to be on the safe side.

"Now, Cole," Brock said, "It isn't polite to start shooting the place down."

"Fuck politeness," Cole remarked back in a dry voice, popping a clip out of the gun and slamming in another.

"Yeah, politeness gets you shit," Drake added coldly, looking around the room and doing the same thing with his gun.

"And we don't have time for it," Cole added.

One twin looked at the other. The one who didn't seem so harsh shook his head and grinned while he pulled something out of the bag which was hanging over his shoulder. "I told dad that you would be a bad influence on those two."

"Hello, Jada." She jumped and looked up. Cole was leaning over the table, smiling down at her. She didn't even see him move away from the twins. "Glad to see you're still in one piece."

She got to her feet, not once taking her eyes off those two. She pointed at them, "Who are they?"

"One on the left is Drake, who you've talked to a couple times, and the other is Brock," he answered. "I'd cover your ears."

Brock lit a fuse on the homemade bomb. He waited a few seconds before he threw it across the room.

"And you are so much better," Drake said to Brock.

Brock smiled, covered his ears and turned away seconds before it exploded. "I could've been."

"Guys!" Cole yelled. "Later. Please!"

Drake looked from Cole to Brock. "He has a point."

"Yeah, he does," Brock agreed. "We can finish this later on, little brother."

Drake growled before he went a different way. "Only by two fucking minutes."

Jada turned to leave, but Cole grabbed a hold of her arm, stopping her. "Where do you think you're going?"

"Let me go Cole," she tried to yank her arm free, but he didn't let go.

"Jada—" Cole didn't get to finish what he was going to say. She kicked him in the leg, he let go, and she took off running out the door. "Jada!" he yelled.

* * * *

Cole was about to go after her, but Drake's voice stopped him: "Let her go. We can get her ass later. We need to find them before this whole place goes up and the cops come."

He didn't like the thought of letting her go. In fact, it pissed him off. That was twice now she had run from him when he needed information she had, and he made himself a promise right there. There was *not* going to be a third time.

"Got him!" Brock yelled.

Cole turned and headed over to Brock who was kneeling down next to a very large man. It had to be Kane. And just looking at him Cole saw the similarity between Drake and him. It was definite by the dark looks and body build. Drake was his father.

"Where's the girl?" Cole asked.

"I don't know," Brock shook his head. "Drake help me here!" he yelled over to Drake. "He's damn heavy."

Cole looked around and spotted the cages the two had been held in. One was empty but the other wasn't. He rushed to it and couldn't get over what he saw.

A pale young girl who looked to be about fourteen or fifteen sat on a steel cot hugging her knees to her chest and hiding her face. She was shaking and her pale blonde hair covered her face. Inside with her was another guy, out cold on the floor face down. Cole looked around for something that might help him get the door opened.

He saw nothing.

"You're not going to believe it. I found another guy over here!" Cole yelled.

Shifters 5: Cole's Awakening

Cole closed his eyes, took several deep breaths and released part of his animal side. Strength came to him quickly and when he grabbed onto the cage door and pulled, the thing popped open. He went inside, rolling the guy over to his back. He was out cold, his face showing one hell of a beating.

"Give him here." Brock came up behind him, reaching for the guy. He pulled him out, leaving Cole with the girl.

"Give me your hand!" Cole yelled, reaching for her. But she shook her head no and tried to get as far away from him as she could get. Clearly, she was afraid of people and he didn't blame her for a second. "Sasha! Take my hand!"

Shaking, Sasha finally raised her head and reached out for the hand. Cole yanked her out, wrapping his arm around her tightly. When she stumbled and almost fell he picked her up, swung her around into his arms. She held on tight and he was able to run out.

He got out just in time. Part of the ceiling that had caught on fire thanks to Brock's little bomb caved in. It just happened to be in the same spot Sasha's cage was located. Still holding her tight, Cole watched with Drake and Brock as the building went up in flames.

"I think Dad said it once, but I'll say it again," Brock remarked. "The war has started."

"It started years ago." Drake was on the ground watching the fire, Kane draped over his lap passed out. "But this…" He took a deep breath, looked down and touched Kane gently on the face. "Is unforgivable. They're going to pay for this."

"They will, Drake," Cole said. "Oh they will."

Epilogue

It had been almost a week since Cole went with the brothers to get Kane and Sasha out, as well as Brandon Michael. Brandon had stumbled upon Josh Stan by pure accident. He'd been traveling and was heading back home. He stopped for the full moon and was taken. He was beaten because he refused to have sex with Sasha. Apparently, because she had a strange birthmark on her shoulder, Josh wanted to test if she could breed or not after all. It had Kane going into a rage, which gave Jason a reason to beat him.

Cole just shook his head over it all. He didn't understand any of it. But what he was looking forward to and understood was going back home with Celine. After discussing it with her parents and with Dedrick's understanding that Cole was on their side, Celine was going to go back to school. Cole was welcomed to stay at the house during that time, but he let them know he was going to start a business of his own in the town. A carpenter/wood working shop. They had a plan, and Cole was sure without a doubt that he and Celine would be able to handle it all. By the third week, Cole was ready to head back to the mountains. When he got up Drake and Carrick were already gone. They took Kane and Sasha with them up to the mountains.

Cole didn't envy Drake one bit. He had a job on his hands with those two. Both were afraid to trust, and no one could blame them. Drake had this urge to fill a void for them and to fix the wrong which had been done to them, but had no clue as to how to go about it. Cole didn't look forward to Kane up in the woods. The large man scared the shit out of him.

True to all they'd been told about Kane, he was more animal than man. He didn't trust anyone, and protected Sasha like a mamma dog with her pups.

"Hey, it's time to head home." Cole walked into Chase's room only to stop with a frown and look around. Chase wasn't in the room. "Chase?" He went inside, looked into the bathroom and then the closet. Everything was gone.

"He left early this morning." Jaclyn stood in the doorway. "He wanted me to give you this, since I was up when he left."

Cole walked over to her, taking the letter from her hand.

Hey man,

Don't get upset. I left with Brandon. Cole, I need some time alone, need to stand on my own two feet for a change. You're always there when I need you, just like you promised when mom and dad died. So please understand when I say I need this. I need to put space between me and someone else before I do something stupid. Try not to worry about me. I'll write. Let you know where I'm at and what's going on.

Now you can use my place if you want, but you two have to stay out of my room. Don't need none of that lovey dovey crap going on in my own bed.

I don't know how long I'm going to be gone. I just know I need to do this for me, and for her. Please understand.

Chase.

"Her?" Cole frowned. He looked up at Jaclyn. "What the hell is going on here?"

Jaclyn shrugged. "He told me he just needed to put space between him and someone else. So I'm going to take it that he found his mate and she's young."

"But to leave?" Quickly he reread the letter, not understanding any of it. "It doesn't make sense. He has a place of his own and now he's leaving it."

"He isn't a little boy Cole." That had him looking back up at her. "Chase is a man, and like all of you guys, human and shifter, you have to go out and do what you think is right. If Chase has the urge to go out and see the world, let him. Don't stand in his way because you don't want to lose him."

"When the hell did you get to be so wise?" he smirked.

Jaclyn smiled and put her arm around his shoulders, walking with him out of the room and down the stairs. "Oh I've always known what the hell I've been talking about. Just the men in this house tend to be too stubborn to hear shit."

After a big breakfast, they were leaving. Cole wanted to have Celine all to himself before coming back here for her schooling. One more month and he was going to have to share her again. One rule though he told her in front of her parents was that the weeks of finals he wasn't going to be here at the house. She was to focus only on her studies, not him. Dedrick agreed, even after Celine put on her pout. He also reminded her about the bakery she wanted to start.

Sidney kissed him good-bye, Stefan shook his hand and Jaclyn hugged him tightly, crying softly. When he went up to Dedrick, Cole got that all nervous feeling again. The man could break him in half if he wanted to, and it was a wonder to him why he didn't. Hell his damn jaw still hurt when he thought about the confrontation he had with the man as soon as he found out that Cole had known for ten years Celine was his mate.

Cole stuck his hand out to Dedrick, hoping like hell he wasn't going to get hit again. "Thanks for everything."

Dedrick looked down at the hand, his eyes narrowed and Cole just knew he was going to get hit again. In fact, he was expecting it. What he wasn't expecting was for Dedrick to take his hand and pull him in to a tight hug.

"You take care of my little girl," Dedrick said in his ear. "She's my world."

Cole stood back when Dedrick released him. He met the other man's eyes. "She's my heart and soul. Nothing will ever happen to her. I promise."

He nodded. "I'll hold you to your promise. Because the day you ever hurt her, I'm going to kill you."

The corner of his mouth went up, but he didn't smile. "I can live with that."

Dedrick slapped him on the back. "Good, now go and help Drake out with our new family members. He's going to need it with Kane."

* * * *

Jada snuck into an abandoned lab she had found months ago in the dead of the night. The place was a mess, smashed to hell. Perfect for her to hide things that she didn't want anyone else to find. Which is what she did weeks ago and now she needed to move.

She made her way back to the office and went right up to the wall, looking for the switch to the hidden wall she had found the first time she was here. And inside that was a built in small freezer that still worked.

She found it, pressed against the wall and a hidden door popped open. Jada smiled at the freezer. It looked just like the ones in a hospital, only smaller.

She opened the door and grabbed the container that was sitting alone. This is what they were willing to kill for, and it didn't stop her from taking it either. She put it in the small cooler that she brought, turned, and got the hell out of there. She had what she came for, now all she had to do was find another place to hide until it all cooled down.

* * * *

Celine rested her head on Cole's shoulder.

"Now tell me again what he said?" Cole asked.

He was referring to Kane. Celine had been with Drake when Kane woke up. Kane had been out for two days. It was strange, only because of the information they had about his strength and determination. He wasn't the kind to pass out from a severe beating or drugs. Only after they were all up here did Sasha finally speak, and it was to Drake. All she said was that they were safe and Kane knew it, which was why he was resting. He finally was able to let his body heal. But that wasn't what shocked Drake.

When Kane did open his eyes, he looked right into Drake's eyes and spoke. Celine was helping with the bandaging of his back and the dead, emotion in his eyes broke her heart. Kane was a beaten man and if luck was on his side, finally, then he was going to need time and patience from the family in order for him to mend. However, that wasn't why a chill went down Drake and Celine's backs.

"You're like me," Kane whispered with a frown at Drake. "You're my father."

Even now, telling Cole, Celine shivered in his arms. "I don't understand how he knew that," she said. "He just looked at Drake and knew that he was his father. Creepy."

"What did Drake do?"

She chuckled and reared up, resting her head on her hand and looked down at him. "I think it was the first time I've ever seen him pale. I swear he freaked out."

Cole smiled, "I would have loved to have seen that."

"Oh, don't you worry, I'm sure you're going to see it plenty of times." She ran her hand down the middle of his chest, under the sheet and cupped him. Cole sucked his breath in and reared his back. "But at the moment I would like for you to see me only." She slid over him, parting his legs for her body. She licked his nipple, "I missed you."

He bit his lower lip and stared down at her, "How much?"

Celine took hold of his tight boxers and pulled them down his hips as she slid down his body. Taking hold of his engorged cock, she stroked it lovingly then kissed the head, licking the precome from the tip.

"Are you trying to put me in an early grave?" he asked with a slight pant to his words.

She stopped and batted her eyes at him, putting her best 'I didn't do it' expression on. "You don't like it?"

Cole chuckled and rubbed his hands over his face quickly. "Never said that, but this light teasing shit is going to be the death of me."

"Ahhhh." She licked the underside from balls to tip. "Poor baby."

Cole growled and the sound vibrated all the way to her throbbing clit. Celine smiled again right before she opened her lips and took him into her mouth. She sucked as hard as she could, pulling on the ridged flesh, drawing another taste from his slit. It was addictive, his taste. Almost like a drug that had her pussy weeping for fulfillment.

"I'm not going to last." Cole breathed hard when she cast a quick glance up at him. "I'm so fucking close."

Somehow, he got her to stop. The flesh she was enjoying very much was taken from her mouth and he dragged her up his body. A hot, demanding kiss and thrusting tongue replaced it and Celine moaned. She straddled him, pulled back, and with eyes locked with him, she pulled the long night shirt she was wearing over her head and tossed it behind her. Taking hold of his shaft, Celine rubbed the head up and down against her slit, but didn't let him slip inside her. She enjoyed the feeling of his scalding heat rubbing against her.

"Son of a bitch," Cole gasped. "You are so damn hot."

Both of his hands came up to her breasts, cupping her as she lowered herself down on him. He stretched and filled her, sending chills of pleasure down her spine along with a hunger for more.

Celine didn't wait one minute. The second she was completely filled, she was moving. She held onto his wrists and moved her hips fast and hard. This time Celine fucked him and took everything he had, demanding more and more.

Quicker, harder, she pounded on him until a scream tore from her lips and her pussy clamped down with her orgasm. She couldn't control her movements and was thankful when Cole flipped her on her back and finished it. The urgency for release was apparent with the powerful, almost brutal manner in which he thrust into her.

One climax turned into another before Cole yelled, reared back, and clamped his mouth over her shoulder, biting the mark he'd left. She felt him swell inside her, felt the hot spurts of his seed and tightened her arms and legs around him.

"I love you, Cole," she sighed in his ear.

Cole released her shoulder and sat up just enough to look down at her. He kissed the tip of her nose, his eyes softening. "I've loved you, Celine Draeger, since the first time I laid eyes on you. And from this night on I'm going to make damn sure I show you just how much every day of my life."

She gave him her biggest smile. "I'm going to hold you to it."

He chuckled and kissed her deep before sliding out of her body and scooping her in his arms. "Now get some sleep. We have our work cut out for us between my brother and your new cousins."

She snuggled up against him and yawned. "Cole?"

"Humm."

"You know when I said I would live with you in a tent. I was just being rhetorical right?"

He chuckled, keeping his eyes closed. "You said it, baby, I'm just delivering it."

"Okay, but how long do we have to stay in the tent?" She glanced up hearing the first drop of rain. True to his word, Cole pitched a tent on his ground and told her that was where they were going to stay until he had a house built.

"Until you learn not to scream so loud when you come," he teased. "You're very loud you know."

She sighed, "Well, I guess for at least the rest of the summer then. But don't expect me to sleep in one when we get to my parents. I have a plan to tie you to my bed."

He smiled. "I'll look forward to that."

She snuggled close, resting her head on his shoulder. With a smile, she closed her eyes and relaxed. Finally, she had him and Celine planned on never letting him go.

*** *

www.jadensinclair.com

Also by Jaden Sinclair at www.melange-books.com:

Interplanetary Passions
Outerplanetary Sensations
S.E.T.H.
S.H.I.L.O.
Lucifer's Lust, with Mae Powers

In the Shifter Series:
Book 1: Stefan's Mark
Book 2: Claiming Skyler
Book 3: Dedrick's Taming
Book 4: The Prowling
Book 5: Cole's Awakening
Book 6: The New Breed
Book 7: Seducing Sasha

The New Breed
By Jaden Sinclair

Kane is a one of a kind shifter. He's more animal than man. Tortured all his life, beaten and experimented on. He has very little tolerance for anyone, except for his twin sister.

Jada Leonard is a woman who never followed anyone's rules but her own, but those rules change when she is caught spying and taking information. To save her life she is forced into hiding and forced to follow rules.

Like a match to gas, these two ignite a fire of passion. Both are strong willed and both refuse to bend. Will Kane give in to his instincts and take what belongs to him? Or will Jada be the one to make the new breed bow down, showing him that he's more than just an animal inside?

Lightning Source UK Ltd.
Milton Keynes UK
UKOW08f1435010517

300253UK00002BA/601/P